CLASS RING

Josephine Wunsch

D0818695

SCHOLASTIC INC.
New York Toronto London Auckland Sydney Tokyo

Cover Photo by Owen Brown

ISBN 0-590-32359-8

12 11 10 9 8 7 6 5 4 3   3 4 5 6/8

Printed in the U.S.A.   06

CLASS RING

A Wildfire Book

WILDFIRE TITLES
FROM SCHOLASTIC

Love Comes to Anne by Lucille S. Warner
I'm Christy by Maud Johnson
That's My Girl by Jill Ross Klevin
Beautiful Girl by Elisabeth Ogilvie
Superflirt by Helen Cavanagh
A Funny Girl Like Me by Jan O'Donnell
Just Sixteen by Terry Morris
Suzy Who? by Winifred Madison
Dreams Can Come True by Jane Claypool Miner
I've Got a Crush on You by Carol Stanley
An April Love Story by Caroline B. Cooney
Dance with Me by Winifred Madison
One Day You'll Go by Sheila Schwartz
Yours Truly, Love, Janie by Ann Reit
The Summer of the Sky-Blue Bikini
  by Jill Ross Klevin
I Want to Be Me by Dorothy Bastien
The Best of Friends by Jill Ross Klevin
The Voices of Julie by Joan Oppenheimer
Second Best by Helen Cavanagh
A Kiss for Tomorrow by Maud Johnson
A Place for Me by Helen Cavanagh
Sixteen Can Be Sweet by Maud Johnson
Take Care of My Girl by Carol Stanley
Lisa by Arlene Hale
Secret Love by Barbara Steiner
Nancy & Nick by Caroline B. Cooney
Wildlife Double Romance by Diane McClure Jones
Senior Class by Jane Claypool Miner
Cindy by Deborah Kent
Too Young to Know by Elisabeth Ogilvie
Junior Prom by Patricia Aks
Saturday Night Date by Maud Johnson
He Loves Me Not by Caroline Cooney
Good-bye, Pretty One by Lucille S. Warner
Just a Summer Girl by Helen Cavanagh
The Impossible Love by Arlene Hale
Sing About Us by Winifred Madison
The Searching Heart by Barbara Steiner
Write Every Day by Janet Quin-Harkin
Christy's Choice by Maud Johnson
The Wrong Boy by Carol White
Make A Wish by Nancy Smiler Levinson
The Boy For Me by Jane Claypool Miner
Class Ring by Josephine Wunsch

ONE

"Sherry," the homeroom teacher stopped by the back desk. "Miss Hatcher wants to see you."

"Me?" Sherry straightened.

"Right now. In her office."

Why me? Sherry asked herself. Nervously, she rifled through her open notebook as if somewhere among the equations, charts, and quotations she could find the answer to the unexpected summons.

"You're excused," Ms. Martin said, and Sherry knew she should hurry. She pocketed the blue slip, and running the gauntlet of curious eyes, she went out into the empty hall.

Her heels clicked over the linoleum. *Me . . . me . . . me . . . why me?* She hadn't skipped school. She hadn't cheated. Why had the principal sent for her? Miss Hatcher, the

Hatchet Lady. The lady with the big stick. The lady who got her jollies cutting down big kids to bite-size.

"Dad," she'd told her father last fall, "as a member of the school board, you've got to ease Miss Hatcher into early retirement. She's a sadist. All the kids hate her."

"Not all, Sherry. Miss Hatcher keeps a tight ship and is stricter than most, but she runs a fine school, and really goes to bat for the kids who can't afford college."

"Hard to believe."

"I know, but it's true. She's asked me for a scholarship donation on more than one occasion. We're very proud of her record. Not another town in the whole of Michigan the size of Pineridge has so many students admitted to college, and the best colleges at that. Take the university —"

"*Forget* the university. Who wants to go hundreds of miles away to that monster when there's a great little college close by?" Close enough so she could come home weekends and be with Kent Halliday.

"With your good grades," Dad said, "when the time comes you may decide to try for something more challenging."

"Never."

Sherry stopped her daydreaming and quickened her pace down the hall. She touched the blue slip in her pocket, and like a gas flame, it ignited a slow burn deep within her. She hated the Hatchet House, as everyone called Miss Hatcher's office.

Hurry, she told herself. Miss Hatcher does not take kindly to waiting. But why hurry to the hangman? She passed by her locker and the locker next to it, which belonged to her best friend, Tina Trowbridge. She moved on to Room 101, glancing through the glass pane in the top of the closed door, hoping — her heart quickened at the sight of the dark hair tumbling in disarray over the high forehead. At the same moment she saw him, Kent looked up from his book and saw her. His long face, so serious in repose, lighted up into a thousand shining watts, and Sherry smiled, too. He had felt her presence through a closed door. Tina would call it ESP. But Sherry knew it for what it was — *love*. Her hand flew to the ring she was wearing on a gold link chain around her throat, a constant reminder of her seventeenth birthday — a month ago today — when she and Kent had exchanged rings.

"Oh, Kent, do you mean it?" She hadn't expected a ring so soon.

"Have I ever said what I didn't mean?"

"But the engraving. *Always*. That's a long time."

He shrugged his lean shoulders. "Hasn't it always been just the two of us?" He took her hand in his and smoothed back her hair, which was as light and silky as his was heavy and dark. "When you have something good going, why change things?"

Why, indeed!

Mom always said, "Don't rush into marriage. Marriage is for life." But when she had shown Mom the ring with the inscription, *Always*, Mom had given her a hug. "We're so fond of Kent, and isn't it wonderful you'll be staying right here in Pineridge?"

Now Sherry's eyes met Kent's through the glass partition and she waved, but he was sitting in the front row and couldn't wave back. He managed a wink, however, before lowering his head over his book. She set off along the hall, knowing that he was thinking of her just as she was thinking of him. She would not let Miss Hatcher get to her. What did it matter? Spring was here. One more year at Pineridge High and she'd be free, free to go away or free to stay and marry Kent. When she saw him tonight . . .

Tonight, last night, every day. All their lives they had been together. Her mother and his mother had taken turns wheeling the two of them in the same carriage. She had talked first, but he had walked first and had grown tall and strong at an early age, while she had been plagued by allergies and attacks of croup. She had made him his first valentine, all stuck with paste, and he had made her a snowman. Dad had a fit when he found his meerschaum pipe impaled in the snow. She had asked him to a leap year dance and then had to teach him to dance before she could take him; he had asked her to her first horror show and when she'd shrieked he held her hand through the scary parts.

Sherry sobered. His lovely mother had died so young. After the funeral Mom had put her arm around the weeping, bewildered boy and said, "Come back home with us, Kent," and he'd stayed until his grieving father had recovered sufficiently to care for him.

A year later his father married a young widow he'd met at the hospital when Kent's mother was dying. Kent had gone to pieces. "How could he? Lolly's no more like Mom than a dandelion's like a rose." In rapid succession three little stepsisters had been born, and with each birth Kent gravitated more and more to Sherry's house. He made a habit of dropping by every evening and Mom told him he was always welcome at meals. He took Mom up on the offer. "Lolly cooks out of a can and Dad's not much better. Everything tastes so good over here." He fitted into the family circle and as time went by he and Sherry became close friends — until, at fifteen, friendship miraculously blossomed into love.

Sherry suddenly stopped at Miss Hatcher's office. She teetered on the threshold, putting all thought of Kent behind her before opening the door. The secretary pounced on her.

"Miss Hatcher is expecting you."

The inner office was a small square room, with gray walls studded with diplomas and potted plants along the sunny sill. As Tina put it, "Miss Hatcher loves plants, but hates kids." There was a huge desk, and behind it

Miss Hatcher swiveled her chair around to face Sherry.

"Sit down, Sherry." Miss Hatcher indicated a straight-backed chair. Only then did Sherry notice the girl curled up in the big leather chair in the corner, her breathing deep and rhythmic like waves lapping a shore. How was it that this girl could relax and sleep under Miss Hatcher's eagle eye, when the mere thought of facing the Hatchet Lady had sent Sherry into a state of irrational panic?

"Wake up! Wake up!" Miss Hatcher banged a paperweight on the desk. The snow in the Swiss village flurried.

The girl yawned and stretched. She was not pretty. Her eyes were enormous in her small face, and the snub nose and the hair — no girl in Pineridge had her hair cropped so short — gave her a pixie look. If she were here for a time, maybe she'd catch on and let it grow. The girl yawned again. "Jet lag," she said. "Worse coming home from England than going over, wouldn't you say, Mrs. Cratchett?"

The cords stood out on Miss Hatcher's neck. "The name is *Hatcher*. And I would like to be properly addressed as *Miss*."

"Oh" — the girl looked more surprised than repentant — "you're not married. My mum's on her third husband, and she said this one is the best of the lot."

Sherry gasped. Who was this girl who dared to speak like this to the principal of Pineridge High?

"I am not the least interested in your mother's marital adventures," Miss Hatcher said coldly. "That's her problem. You are my problem."

"I'm only here because Mum said if anything went amiss, I should go to the school or to the police. I tossed a coin. You won."

The chair swiveled. Miss Hatcher bit off her words as if addressing a not-too-bright child. "I have been in touch with Sherry's father, who is on the school board, and we have come up with a plan for you. You will go home with Sherry until your grandmother is located." She sniffed. "How your mother could put you on a transatlantic flight until firm arrangements had been made —"

The girl sprang to her feet. Sherry had to admit she was agile. "I told you Gam *is* expecting me. It's just that the plans got changed. Mum and Sir — that's what my new stepfather wants me to call him — they had to leave for Singapore sooner than they expected. We tried to reach Gam by phone, but her phone is on the blink." She cocked her head, and her big eyes challenged. "Do you have a lot of trouble with your phones around here?"

"Nothing whatsoever is the matter with the *school* switchboard."

The girl arched a brow. "Gam's sort of a bird. Perhaps she forgot to pay her bill."

Sherry leaned forward. "Who is your grandmother?"

Simultaneously Miss Hatcher and the girl

turned to look at Sherry, and she had the feeling that they had forgotten she was there.

"Mrs. Williams," the girl said. "Dolly Williams."

"I don't know her," Sherry said. "But I bet Mom does. Mom knows everyone."

Miss Hatcher recovered. "I don't believe you two have met. Sherry Russell, this is Jill Keller. Jill is a nickname, I presume, for Gillian."

"Jill's for real. Mum said you can waste half your life signing your name — all those government forms — so by giving me a name with only four letters she was doing me a favor, and I'm thinking of dropping an *l* to make it three. Who needs a monstrosity like Jacqueline or —"

The bell rang. Instant pandemonium. Banging lockers. Shouts. Laughter.

Miss Hatcher rose, glancing with distaste at the stack of suitcases behind her desk. "Mr. Russell will stop for your luggage on his way home from the bank. He will then deliver you and your bags to your grandmother's. At least I trust by then the missing Mrs. Williams will have shown up and will assume her family responsibilities."

"You worry too much," Jill said. "Gam's bound to show up sometime."

"And if she hasn't shown up by dinner," Miss Hatcher said acidly, "I'll expect a call from your mother, Sherry."

Jill giggled. "The worst that can happen, I'll be running the streets of Pineridge for a

8

couple of months until I get the word to fly on to Singapore."

"A couple of months —" Miss Hatcher pressed the palms of her hands against her temples. She closed her eyes and grimaced as if a thousand hammers were beating at her skull.

"Good-bye, Miss Hatcher," Sherry said politely, and turned toward the door.

Once beyond the school grounds, Sherry collapsed on the curb. She laughed, doubling over until her head touched her kneecaps. She laughed until her sides ached and tears ran in rivulets down her cheeks.

"What's so funny?" Jill leaned back against a maple. The trunk was tinged with pink and tight new leaves curled on the twigs.

"Jill — you're a hero! I can't wait to tell the gang. They won't believe anyone had the I.F. to stand up to Miss Hatcher. Oh, they call her the Hatchet Lady behind her back, but when the office door closes it's 'yes, ma'am' and 'no, ma'am' and 'as you suggest, Miss Hatcher, twenty days of detention is just fine with me.'"

"What's I.F?" Jill said.

"Intestinal fortitude. Guts."

Jill shrugged. Lithe muscles rippled in the thin shoulders. "I've been to a dozen different schools with a dozen different headmistresses, and odd's on that old fossil Hatcher is a pushover."

"Don't you ever believe it." Sherry jumped

up from the curb and pointed to the Ridge. "See! We're the white house behind the windbreak of pine. Mom'll be expecting us."

They started up the hill side by side. Sherry felt the sun on her back and a warm glow deep inside her. She had just made a fabulous new friend.

TWO

Halfway up the hill Jill fell silent. Her gray green eyes took on a faraway look and little worry wrinkles webbed the corners, and Sherry felt concerned.

"A penny for your thoughts," she said.

Jill turned her head slowly, blinking. "Sorry, I'm not with it. What did you say?"

"Just wondering what's on your mind. You freaked out in the middle of a sentence."

"What sentence?"

"Hope Miss Hatcher didn't get to you."

"Oh, no. Not that old windbag."

"Then it has to be your grandmother." Sherry's voice deepened with compassion.

Jill shrugged. "It would be nice knowing I had a roof over my head."

"Don't worry," Sherry said in a burst of generosity, "you can always spend the night with me."

"That would be super!"

No sooner had Sherry offered than she regretted it. All very well to be hospitable, but what if Mom wouldn't go along? Overnight, maybe. An emergency situation. But Mom would never take Jill in on a long-term basis. Sherry felt a cold stone in the pit of her stomach. What happened to a strange girl in a strange town? There was no place to go in Pineridge. No room at the inn.

But the mere offer of a place for the night had a cheering effect. Jill walked faster and her smile brightened. Sherry brightened, too, and she decided to do what she could to keep Jill's mind off the fix she was in.

"Now you can see why it's called Pineridge!" Sherry stopped at the top of the hill and gestured toward the row of trees stretching along the edge of the Ridge in an exact line.

"Not as nice as England!" Jill scoffed, but she tilted her head and looked up at the dark green treetops swaying against the bright blue sky.

Realizing that she had sparked Jill's interest, Sherry warmed to her subject. "They're white pines and very old, and the houses on the Ridge are old, too. They were built by the lumber barons back in the days when the great forests were being lumbered off."

"Like when?"

"Like over a hundred years ago."

Jill guffawed. "In England, a hundred years is but a day. New Forest is so old William the Conqueror used it as his hunting grounds, and a house has to be lived in for forty generations before it's worth noticing." Jill spread her small, square hands, palms up. "But I think I'm going to like it here. A town that's old but not ancient. Befriended by Sherry of the House of Russell on the Ridge."

"I know you'll like it here," Sherry said fervently, swinging her book bag over her shoulder. "It's such a neat place. Mom and I were just talking about it the other day. Not everyone is lucky enough to grow up in a beautiful northern town that isn't overrun with tourists."

"What's the catch?"

"We're too far from Lake Michigan for the summer invasion and too far from the mountains for the skiers." Sherry skip-hopped over a crack in the sidewalk. She knew every crack in town. "And when the big exodus from Detroit began, there were no job openings, so thankfully the world passed us by." Sherry took a deep breath of the spice-scented air. "I just can't imagine living in any other place."

"I can't count all the places I've lived," Jill said with a shrug, but Sherry noticed the fleeting shadow that darkened the luminous eyes. "All over Europe. And probably Singapore next."

Sherry wanted to reach out and comfort her new friend. No roots. A tumbleweed blown hither and yon and accidentally blown into Pineridge. But when she spoke her voice was matter-of-fact.

"Turn here, Jill. Back Road." A high stockade fence on one side barricaded the big homes from the road, and on the other side a pine woods ringing with bird songs stretched along the road as far as the meadow. "If the road seems bumpy to you, we keep it that way to discourage traffic."

"Not to worry," Jill said, leaping from rut to hump, as light on her feet as a ballet dancer.

She looked so eager running ahead—running ahead to what? Sherry wondered. An alien land, steamy hot down by the equator, with a stepfather called Sir instead of Dad.

Sherry sighed. There wasn't anything she could do about Singapore, but at least she could see to it that Jill's stay in Pineridge would be fun.

"I want you to meet all my friends," Sherry told Jill, "and have a great time here so when you're far away in Singapore, you'll have happy memories of all of us."

"Really?" Jill sounded skeptical.

"I wouldn't say it if I didn't mean it."

"I'm surprised, that's all. Mom said most Michigan towns were friendly, but Pineridge was something else. Unless you'd lived here forever, you were an outsider."

"That's not true!" Sherry said emphatically. But try as she would she couldn't come up with anyone new to town that she'd ever befriended, and with her eye on Jill she resolved to remedy the oversight.

Standing on tiptoe, Jill craned to see over the high fence. "Which is your place, Sherry?"

"You're looking in Mrs. Brophy's yard. She's a darling old lady who lives all by herself in that huge house. We're next door. And the barn across the road in the middle of the meadow, that's ours."

"Horses?" Jill said. "I'm mad about horses."

"You're a little late. We haven't had horses for ages. Oh, I had a pony when I was a kid, and Dad even built a ring. But I outgrew the pony and the ring is gone. Now the barn is a garage, and the tack room's a meeting place for all the guys on the Ridge, the Block Club."

"Block Club?" Jill straightened, instantly alert.

"I'll tell you all about it some other time," Sherry said. If only Jill belonged! In no time at all she'd know everyone. But she couldn't discuss the Club with Jill yet. She pulled the latchstring on the gate and stepped inside the spacious yard, the old lilac bushes taller than the fence and the center circle of roses deep in peat moss showing signs of greening.

"Your home," Jill said, "it's lovely."

Sherry smiled. Jill, who had been everywhere and seen everything, loved the old homestead just as she herself loved it. Suddenly it seemed important that Jill enter by the front door rather than through the back hall, which was always a jumble of coats and clutter.

Sherry waved. "This way. We'll go in the front."

"One-two-three-four," Jill counted as she walked along the side of the house. "Four stories. That's amazing."

"The top floor is closed off," Sherry said. "You can tell by all the nests along the sills. The barn swallows come back year after year knowing they won't be disturbed. But we still use the third floor. Mother's sewing room is up there and when Aunt Cornelia comes from Texas for her summer visit, she prefers the privacy of the third floor."

"Where's your room?" Jill asked.

"Second floor front, the one with the shutters and big window. If you spend the night you'll be in the guest room and we'll have an adjoining bath."

"I can't wait," Jill said. "We'll stay up late and chat every night."

The happy timbre of her voice chilled Sherry. This very instant she should make it clear that the invitation was for one night only. But she didn't want Jill to worry again. Shielding her eyes from the onslaught of sun, Sherry looked out over the Ridge. "See the steeple?" she said. "That's the highest landmark on Main Street. Right below us is Pineridge High —"

Jill wasn't looking or listening. "Why have

you the only house on the Ridge with a fence out front?"

"Oh, that. Dad put it up after my fall. I was just two when I fell over the edge and half-way down the embankment before a bush caught me. I wasn't hurt, only bruised, but the fall left its mark. Mom says that's why I panic at heights. Are you afraid of high places?"

"No. I'd take up hang-gliding if I had a chance."

Sherry gave Jill a sidewise glance. She had to be kidding. "I won't even watch those idiots on TV," she said, and turned toward the house.

The wide front hall with its bronze chandelier, golden oak staircase, and stained-glass window on the landing usually impressed visitors. Sherry waited by the newel post and wondered what Jill would have to say. But Jill hung back, staring at a framed watercolor by the door.

"Looks familiar," she said.

Sherry smiled indulgently. "Don't you see it's this house? Only in the picture there's a porch across the front, and that makes the difference. Some long-gone ancestor painted it on the Fourth of July, 1897, and it's a good thing she did. Right after that a tornado blew through town and ripped off the front porch."

"Gam never mentioned any tornado."

"The tornado was a freak. Never one before. Never one since. It did a lot of damage, but at least some good came out of it. Along with the porch, the outhouse blew away, and from that time on we've had indoor plumbing."

"Anything for progress," Jill said.

"Jill, I want you to meet my mother." Sherry called upstairs. "Mom! Moth-er!"

The reply came from the back of the house. "I'm in the kitchen, dear."

Sherry led the way down the center hall, past the living room on the left and the dining room on the right, with its paneled walls and corner cupboard stacked with the Blue Willow plates and deep saucers. Sherry cherished them because they'd belonged to her great-great-grandmother and would someday be hers.

The kitchen was huge, an old wood-burning stove with a stovepipe angling like a crooked elbow into the chimney, and a new electric range. Mom was standing over a shining burner stirring a kettle of chili sauce.

How pretty Mom is, Sherry thought. Steam coiled around her, but somehow she still looked trim and cool.

"Yum!" Sherry inhaled and her mouth watered.

Mrs. Russell glanced up from the kettle, stiffening just a little when she saw Jill. The short, shaggy hair, no doubt. It had jolted Sherry at first, too.

"Mom, this is Jill Keller."

"How do you do?" Mom spoke in measured, polite tones.

18

"I do fine," Jill said.

Sherry laughed. How stupid to say "How do you do?" and never expect an answer. But she could tell by the white knuckles on the wooden spoon that Mom didn't appreciate Jill's little joke.

"Would you girls like a snack?" Mom nodded toward the cookie jar. "And help yourself to milk or juice."

"Thanks, Mom."

"Sherry, would you pour me a glass of juice, and then we'll all sit around the breakfast table and talk."

Mom sat down across from Jill. A light breeze from the open window ruffled the gauzy café curtains. A fat robin hopped across the lawn, cocked its head, then drilled its beak into the ground.

"Now, Jill," Mom began, "Miss Hatcher and I are doing our very best to locate your grandmother. We have several lines out, but so far without success. We would appreciate anything you could tell us about her. To start, what does she look like?"

"That depends," Jill said. "The last time I saw her she was a redhead, but the time before that she was a blonde. Sometimes she wears green contact lens and sometimes they're brown. And when her eyebrows are dyed dark she looks one way, but when they're bleached —"

"In other words, it'd do no good to broadcast a description of her." Sherry noted the acid in Mom's usually honeyed voice.

"You could try. But don't be surprised if the wrong person shows up."

Mom drew in a long breath. "Would you by any chance recognize her if we ever find her?"

Jill lifted her chin, making her nose more uptilted than ever. "I would know Gam anyplace," she said.

"She's not at home. We've found out that much from the police."

"That's hardly surprising. She's not the rocking-chair type."

"Is it possible that she has ā job? And if so, what kind of a job?"

"Gam's seen it all — waitress, hostess, beautician, receptionist, dancer, cowgirl." Jill glanced around the room and her knowing eyes settled on Mom. "I bet you haven't had all the fun Gam has had."

"If your grandmother is such ā restless sort," Mom said through pinched lips, "I can't imagine why she'd want to come back to Pineridge."

Jill brightened. "That's ā good question. If we ever find her, we can ask her."

"*Please*, Mom," Sherry pressed forward. "You can stop the third degree. It isn't Jill's fault that her grandmother is among the missing. If you ask me, she's very brave under the circumstances."

Mom wiped her forehead that looked hotter now than it had when she'd been standing over the burner. "Run along," she said.

"C'mon, Jill," Sherry said, "we'll watch the tube until dinner's ready."

"In England it's the telly and umbrellas are brollies —"

Sherry laughed as she ushered Jill into the small den that winged out beyond the living room.

"Oh, so cozy," Jill's eyes flicked over the floor to ceiling bookcases, the leather-top desk, leather couch and chairs, and TV on the stand.

"That's the way we feel about it." Sherry leaned back on the couch. "Kent and I always study in here."

"Kent?" Jill sat down alongside Sherry.

"Kent Halliday. We do everything together." She reached for the ring on the gold chain. "He gave me this on my last birthday."

Jill peered at the ring closely. "No one ever gave me a ring," she said.

"It was a wonderful surprise. Most kids wait until their senior year before they exchange rings."

"You're pretty," Jill said. "Is Kent handsome?"

Sherry felt the color rush to her cheeks. "I think so. Everyone says we're made for each other."

"How can you be sure?"

"If two people have known each other as long as we have they can be sure."

The phone on the desk rang, startling Sherry. She reached over.

"Hello. Yes, she's here." She handed the receiver across to Jill. "It's for you."

"Gam!" Jill shrieked. "Gam, where are you? What a lark!" Jill rocked with laughter. "How did you ever get a job baby-sitting for a household of Siamese cats? No, Gam, I'm not a bit allergic to cats, and I'll be there straight away."

THREE

It had all happened so fast. If anyone had told Sherry that she could make a close friend in two weeks, she wouldn't have believed it. If anyone had told her that she'd be proposing a transient for the Block Club, she wouldn't have believed that either. What's more, Kent and Tina, who knew every move she ever made, had no idea what she was planning for tonight.

Now, waiting for the meeting to begin, doubts nagged her, but she had made Jill a promise last Friday night and she intended to keep it. Jill had asked her to dinner at Gam's, and Sherry had begged off. "The Block Club, you know."

In their conversation, Sherry had explained the Block Club to Jill and explained why Jill couldn't belong, but Jill had said if she ever did belong she would be the best member they'd ever had and would do any old thing

— such as the archives and scrubbing the floors — and it wouldn't hurt to take her in because it would be a temporary thing. Wouldn't Super Sherry give it a go for her?

"I'll do my best," Sherry had said.

Sherry's friends had called her sweet and darling and bright and kind and pretty, but no one ever before had called her Super Sherry.

"I have friends all over the world," Jill had said, "but I'll never have what you call a forever friend, like your Tina and Kent. I've never stayed in one place long enough for that. But some of my quickest friendships have been the longest lasting, and you'll always be Super Sherry, U.S.A."

"We'll write each other," Sherry said. "We'll be the world's busiest pen pals."

"Better than that. Visit me in Singapore."

"Oh, right! It's on the other side of the world."

"Why not? Singapore has all kinds of goodies like alligator farms."

Sherry smiled, amused. The farthest she'd ever been was Washington, D.C., and Dad had made them return home a day early. "We have all the cherry trees anyone needs right here on Grand Traverse Bay."

Sherry had invited Jill to sit at the long table with her friends in the cafeteria. Then, one night when Mom and Dad went out to dinner, Sherry asked Tina, Kent, and Brian over with Jill, and Jill had introduced them to five-card stud. The evening had been a blast.

But that didn't make Jill a candidate for the Block Club. Surely Midge, self-appointed watchdog of the Club, given the chance would organize against Jill. But Sherry had not let on what was up, and Midge would be taken by surprise.

Tina rapped the gavel on the lectern, and Sherry decided that Tina looked even more of a knockout than usual in the white jumpsuit that set off her long, straight blue black hair. "Will the secretary please read the minutes of the last meeting?"

Tubby made his way up onto the platform. Sherry smiled. Tubby had been given his nickname when he was a chunky seventh grader. Now he was the skinniest boy in the senior class — but the nickname stuck.

As Tubby droned on, Sherry moved restlessly on the bench, crossing and recrossing her ankles, twisting her ring on its chain. She was getting jumpier by the minute, even though Kent was so close she could feel his breath on her cheek.

"What's with you?" he whispered.

"Wait."

He gave her a little nudge. "No secrets."

"Will you go along with me?"

"Don't I always?"

She flashed him a grateful smile.

Sherry tuned out, looking around the tack room with pride. The place had been a disaster — mice and spiders, mildew, cobwebs, the splintered floor layered with dust — until she'd talked Dad into letting the gang make it over into a clubhouse. There'd been so many rusty nails that when the renovation began she posted a sign over the door: POSITIVELY NO BARE FEET. SEE YOUR M.D. FOR A TETANUS BOOSTER.

Now it was beautiful. Everyone said so. The wide-beamed boards were sanded and varnished and the walls painted a sunny yellow. On the side wall was a large photograph of the twelve club members, the six boys linking arms with the six girls. A good-looking bunch, all in all. On the opposite wall were photos of the past presidents lined up in a row. Sherry eyed the photo of herself taken at thirteen. How could Kent have ever thought she was the prettiest girl in the class with that mishmash of wires and rubber bands on her teeth?"

"Any new business?"

Sherry jerked forward, raising her hand. What had happened to old business?

"Sherry has the floor." Tina announced in a formal tone. Tina took the presidency seriously. She woke up and went to bed by *Robert's Rules of Order.*

Sherry stepped up onto the podium. Somehow standing even a few inches above the others gave her a sense of authority.

"I would like to propose a new member," she said.

"I didn't know anyone new had moved onto the Ridge," Midge jumped up waving her arms, overreacting as usual. Midge was always first to know about the comings and goings in town — not surprising, since her father was Mr. Big in Pineridge real estate.

Sherry clasped her ring and it gave her new confidence. "I didn't say the person I'm proposing lives on the Ridge."

Tina thumbed through the bylaws. "Right here," she said. "Article 1, Section 2. Membership in the Block Club shall be limited to girls and boys living on the Ridge, ages thirteen to such time as said persons graduate from high school."

Sherry felt the heat rise in her neck. So now her best friend was throwing the rules at her! Thanks for nothing, Tina! And the awful part was that she herself had masterminded these rules.

"Please, you guys," Sherry had said when she'd been the president, "quit the squawking. We're all friends and we want to keep it that way. I herewith appoint a committee to draw up a set of bylaws and guidelines . . ."

Sherry cleared her throat. This was going to be tricky. The antiperspirant touted on TV was doing her no good at all.

"True." She smiled. "The girl I'm proposing doesn't live on the Ridge, but she doesn't live any other place either."

"Are we dealing with a spirit?" A quivering voice from the corner.

Giggles.

Sherry tried to laugh, too, but instead she had a coughing spell and stopped to drink out of the glass that was placed on the lectern for the president.

"I'm referring to a new girl in town." Sherry fought to get herself in control. "She'll only be here a short time, and I for one think it would be a nice gesture to include her in our activities so when she leaves for Singapore —"

"You mean Jill Keller — that new girl you've taken under your wing?" Midge's jaw squared.

"She sure has a crazy haircut," Tubby said.

"It's probably the style in England," Sherry snapped, surprised to hear herself defending the very haircut that she herself thought was pretty weird.

Brian — The Brain — rose. He seldom said anything in meetings. Everyone sat still and listened.

"There have been other transients in Pineridge." He adjusted his glasses, as if waiting for the words to sink in. "Never before have we been concerned where they came from or where they went. Why is this Jill Keller so special?"

He sat down to applause.

Sherry knew this was it. "Jill Keller *is* special," she began. "Who else ever told the Hatchet Lady off?" She went over the conversation in the office and laughed just as hard as she had the day it happened. "Then

Mom gave her the third degree, just like Pineridge was a police state. Now, mind you, she's just off the jet from England and her grandmother is missing and there is no one to meet her and no place to stay. Frankly, if I were in her shoes, stranded in a strange, unfriendly town, I'd be paralyzed." Sherry sighed. "Well, the powers that be have given Jill a really rough time, and I think it's up to us to show her that there are some good guys in Pineridge. Besides," she implored, "Jill is my friend."

Sherry looked out over the room. At least the faces were less hostile than they'd been a moment ago.

Tina said, "Would someone like to make a motion that Jill Keller —"

Midge was on her feet again. "I, for one, am against it."

Tina banged the gavel. "You will have a chance to vote pro or con as you see fit."

Midge plunged on. "We have six boys and six girls. So a newcomer would make an unlucky thirteen. Not only that, but if Jill is accepted, that makes an extra girl at all our doings, and it'll mean odd-girl out."

"Does that scare you all that much?" Sherry's eyes clashed with Midge's.

Tina came down hard on the gavel. "Will someone please make a motion?"

Kent stood up, his face long and sober. Sherry wished he'd turn on his fabulous smile.

"I move that Jill Keller be made a temporary member of the Block Club. No initiation, of course."

Four votes in favor, one against with all other members abstaining. Hardly a howling success, Sherry had to admit, but her mission was accomplished. Jill was in.

"Thanks for making the motion," she told Kent as he walked her home across the road. Her left hand was in his right one, and they swung their arms rhythmically as they moved as one under the starlit sky. His palm was tough and calloused from working in his father's garage, but she loved the way it felt. She looked up at him. "Call me spoiled, but I've always had my way at the Club before. Maybe it's because we meet in our barn and eat Mom's cookies. But they sure gave me a hard time tonight."

"I voted your way, but I didn't want to." He gave her hand a proprietary squeeze. "I think it's a lousy idea to bend the rules. I only went along because you assured me that she'd be here for two months at the most."

"You won't be sorry. She's fun and easy to know. In no time at all you'll be telling me that she's terrific." Sherry smiled. "I'll have to watch out."

"Never." He swung her around and held her close, his lips finding her lips.

FOUR

The Block Club
Cordially invites
Jill Keller
To become a member
For the duration of her stay
In Pineridge.
Meetings Friday evenings at eight.

R.S.V.P.   *Sherry Russell*
                    Corresponding Secretary

Jill Keller
Accepts with glee
Your invitation to be
A member of your
August company.
On Friday nights
Me you'll see.

Sherry read the note and laughed. Today was
Friday, and the note had been left at the

door. Jill wasn't about to miss a single meeting. Sherry had to admit that last week's meeting of the Block Club had jolted her, but she was certain that it was just a matter of time before the members who had risen up against Jill would be telling Sherry what a big plus she was.

Pocketing the note, Sherry skimmed up the wide treads of the carpeted stairs. She paused on the landing to look at the stained-glass window, subdued now in the late afternoon light. This morning the sun had fired up the jewel tones' into vibrant reds and dazzling blues.

Upstairs the ceilings were almost as high as they were downstairs. Sherry poked her head into the half-open door of the master bedroom, which ran the length of the living room. And, like the living room, it had a fireplace with a marble mantel and a bay window. Her eyes reached beyond the four poster with the canopy and dust ruffle, beyond the chaise and the TV, to the corner desk with its cubbyholes and secret drawers where Mom sat, pen in hand.

"Hi," Sherry said, "what are you doing?"

"Writing Aunt Cornelia. She's welcome any time, but I'd like to know the dates."

That's Mom, Sherry thought, *no loose ends*.

"How was your day?" Mom asked, as she always did.

Sherry shrugged. "About now the teachers get fed up, or maybe it's the kids who get fed up, or maybe it's just that the weather's so great that no one wants to be cooped up in a stuffy classroom."

"I know it's close to summer, but don't get lazy," Mom admonished. "Finals will be coming up, and if you want to go to college —"

College. The big stick that her parents and Miss Hatcher held over her head. But now she wondered. Last night Kent had told her that a few night courses at business school were enough for him, so why should she knock herself out preparing for all those college boards? Sherry had always planned to take the college entrance exams, but she didn't want to hassle about it now.

Aloud she said, "Don't forget Block Club. We have to eat early."

"Sherry, dear, have I ever forgotten?"

"Call me the minute Dad gets home."

Sherry turned and walked down the hall to her room, depositing her books on her desk. She opened *The Great Gatsby*, but her eyes traveled from the printed page to the four corners of her room. She'd always liked her room. It wasn't big like the master bedroom, but at night she could look through the windbreak of pine down on the twinkling lights of the town below. And Mom had let her decide on her very own decor. Turquoise walls with white framed pictures; white ruffled curtains with turquoise tiebacks; a brass bed with a turquoise spread; and at the foot of the bed, a cedar chest. Propped on the chest were her favorite animals, Pooh Bear, Flakey, and Jenny the Giraffe. She stared at them and they stared back, and now she knew what was disturbing her.

"What a terrific nursery," Jill had said the first time she'd brought her upstairs, "but where's your room, Sherry?"

Sherry's eyes narrowed. She would talk Mom into redoing it, or better yet she'd do the job herself. It wouldn't take much. Splashy posters on the walls, harem pillows on the bed, possibly an Indian print spread, and a bean bag chair in place of the white rocker.

She caressed the ring. Seventeen and as good as engaged. Time to give up childish things. Determinedly she marched over to the chest and gathered up Pooh Bear and Flakey and Jenny.

"Bye, little friends." She gave them a final hug, and lifting up the lid of the chest, she buried them amid mothballs and winter sweaters.

Now for a mirror check. The mirror surprised her. The room might need a face lift, but she was the same Sherry who had been chosen Homecoming Queen — crowned in gold, robed in purple, and elevated on a throne on the Pineridge High float that had led all the other floats down Main Street. Her light honey hair still shone, her wide apart eyes flashed violet blue, and her smile — well, she'd practiced hours on her smile before riding on that float. No doubt about it — "peaches" did more for her than "cheese."

"Dinner's ready," Mom called upstairs. With a twinge Sherry realized she hadn't made a single note on *The Great Gatsby*, and the paper was due next week.

Dad rose when she walked into the dining room, and when he held out her chair she felt like a princess. He looked dignified in a pin-striped suit — what Sherry called his bank uniform.

"Now tell me all about school," he said, serving up the stew from the Pyrex dish in the silver holder. Mom's stew, with its tender meat and vegetables and pungent herbs, was a far cry from the doctored-up gravy they passed off as stew in the cafeteria.

"Things are okay, except French is a disaster."

"I thought you liked French."

"I don't mean I'm flunking or anything. It's just that Madame Joneau is getting a divorce, and she's acting impossible."

"Madame Joneau? I can't place her."

"Her real name is Jones. She just tacked on the French ending so everyone in her class would learn that 'eau' is pronounced 'oh.'"

"Now I know. She's plump and pretty."

"Right now she's skinny and hopping mad. Tina says that's because she and her husband are breaking up, and she's taking it out on us."

"No one ever said divorces were happy affairs."

"But why should we —"

"Sherry, eat your dinner," Mom said in her not-to-reason-why voice.

"Okay, okay." Sherry helped herself to a chunk of the hot, crusty bread in the basket.

The doorbell rang, and Dad jumped up. "That paper boy should know better than to be collecting in the middle of dinner."

But it wasn't the boy from the *Bugle*. It was Jill.

"Hi," she said when Dad ushered her into the dining room.

"Just got your note a little while ago," Sherry said. "In verse, yet. The guys'll love it."

"I know I'm early. But since this is my first meeting at the Block Club, I didn't want to arrive late or alone." She smiled. "Hope you don't mind taking me, Sherry."

"Of course not. What happened? I didn't see you at school today."

"Gam had to go out of town, so I had the care and feeding of the cats. You see, Gam in her spare time throws pots." Jill giggled. "Not the way it sounds, but on a potter's wheel. There's a street fair in Petoskey, so she's up there — not making a fortune but hopefully enough to keep herself in wigs." She turned to Mom. "I don't suppose that's a wig, Mrs. Russell."

Mom looked startled. "I do not own a wig."

"Pity. You'd be surprised what pink platinum would do for you. Give you a little oomph."

"I've managed to get along all these years without oomph." Mom's voice was ice.

Dad cleared his throat. "Now, Jill, why don't you sit down next to Sherry. I presume you've already eaten —"

"So glad you asked. I haven't eaten, and I'd love some stew."

Mom and Dad exchanged glances.

"Would you bring another plate, Sherry?" Dad said.

Sherry pushed through the swinging kitchen door. She didn't know whether to laugh or to cry. Laugh, because Jill managed to rattle her usually imperturbable parents. Cry, because she wanted Jill for a friend and she could tell her parents were already taking a stand against her. Under the circumstances, it seemed wise to bring a small plate rather than the big dinner kind.

"*Merci beaucoup.*" Jill lifted her fork, and Dad inquired in a conversational tone, "You've taken French?"

"I had no choice. Mother threw me in a convent school in Paris the year Sir — that's my stepfather — was giving Mum the rush."

"I can't picture you in a convent school," Mom said.

"Nor could the nuns," Jill announced between bites. "They tried to give me the chop, but it took them one whole term to locate Mum. By that time Mum had married Sir and I'd learned to speak French, so it wasn't all wasted."

"I see," Mom said, thin-lipped.

Jill pushed the plate aside. "That hit the spot, Mrs. Russell. Any time you get bored, you can always hire yourself out as a cook."

"I am never bored," Mom said, "and what I don't understand is why you have no food in your own house."

"Gam's bringing the groceries from Petoskey. She just wasn't back when I left, but she'll turn up soon." Jill's eyes settled on Mom. "I don't want to give you the wrong impression, Mrs. Russell. There is food in the house — liver and kidneys and smelts, but Gam wouldn't like it if I shortchanged the cats."

Mom stood up suddenly. "I think you girls better run along. And Sherry, the cookies for the Block Club are on the kitchen counter."

"Thanks, Mom. Everyone appreciates —" Sherry dove through the swinging door and waited for Jill who seemed to take forever.

"Don't bother," Jill said when Sherry picked up the cookies. "I have something else in mind."

"Mom baked them, and I'm taking them," Sherry said.

Jill's big eyes got bigger. "How come your mother keeps saying 'run along' as if she can't wait to see the last of us? Is she always that way?"

"Not always." Sherry glanced at the door to the dining room. The truth was Mom welcomed Kent and Tina. Only Jill got Mom's hackles up.

They were the first to arrive at the meeting room. Sherry stowed the cookies in the corner cupboard along with the paper plates and paper cups. Butterflies swooped around her stomach as she busied herself dusting the benches and lectern. She was responsible for Jill. Jill had barely made the Club even though Sherry had put the pressure on. She had to keep Jill in line. With as much tact as she could muster, Sherry said, "It's customary for new members to be seen but not heard. A probation period until the new member is familiar with the rules and regulations."

"Right," Jill said pressing her face against the window. "Here comes Tina. You said she was president?"

"Yes."

"Spanish?"

"She says her great-great-grandmother was an Indian princess. You can see it in her regal bearing and the beautiful black hair."

"She's with Brian."

"Brian Farley, better known as The Brain. He likes Tina and she likes him."

"I get it," Jill said. "The great platonic friendship. Not like you and Kent, the romantic perfect pair."

"There he is now." Sherry leaned forward and the ring grazed the window as she watched Kent lope across the meadow with long, easy strides. She thought of his kiss and how much he meant to her.

In no time at all the room filled up, and

Tina with a rap of the gavel brought order out of chaos.

"Will Sherry please step forward and introduce our new member, Jill Keller?"

Jill and Sherry stepped up on the platform, and Sherry introduced Jill to each member by name.

Sherry stepped down, but Jill didn't follow.

"Sherry told me it was against the rules to say anything," Jill began, and everyone turned and stared at Sherry. She felt color suffuse her neck as Tina thumbed through the bylaws. "Maybe you'll forgive me if I make it short. I only want to say how very happy I am to be a member of your Club. Gam said I could easily have come to Pineridge and left again without meeting one of you. She said Pineridge could be a very lonely place, so I want to thank you for including me, and most especially to thank Sherry for proposing me."

Everyone clapped, and Sherry felt the butterflies fold their wings and rest. Just because Jill antagonized her parents' generation didn't mean that she wouldn't fit into the Block Club. Sherry felt so relieved that when she sat down next to Kent she squeezed his hand and he squeezed hers back.

Tina worked her way through old business. When it came to new business she turned the floor over to Midge.

"Now about the garage sale," Midge rifled through her notes. "We have $179.32 toward the stereo, and it's taken us three years to get that. If we are to reach our goal — a stereo by next Christmas for the dance — we will have to double our efforts. On the basis of past performance, that means each one of us will have to collect twice as many items as last year."

Brian raised his hand. "Objection! Mother said the place was cleaned out last year so I'm absolutely certain —"

Kent said, "Our garage is gross, but Dad won't part with a rusty nail."

Jill was on her feet. "It's mad to mess about with rummage when there's a fool-proof way to raise money."

"Well?" Midge encouraged.

Jill's hand flew to her mouth. "There I go again. Talking too much when I'm on probation."

"Probation?" Tina frowned. Her black eyes flashed storm warnings as they lit into Sherry. "What have you been telling Jill?"

The butterflies flapped. How could she say she was just trying to protect Jill from her enemies within the Block Club when Enemy Number One was now anxious to hear what Jill had to say.

"Go ahead, Jill," Sherry said sweetly.

"At the Academy we called it a sell-yourself-auction. Like Brian — he could sell his ability to write a term paper. Midge could talk her father into letting her house-sit on a Sunday afternoon in a house he has up for sale. And Kent could cut someone else's lawn beside his own."

Kent countered, "And what will you do, Jill?"

"I expect I'll be gone by July, but if not I'd climb the church steeple."

Laughter rippled through the room.

Jill said, "That's it. People would take bets that I couldn't do it, but I really can."

"Just as well we'll never find out." Tina smiled. "Midge and her committee will take your suggestion under advisement, and if the Board decides to proceed with the auction, I hereby appoint Jill Keller to be part of the auction committee." Tina looked around. "Any further business?"

"One more thing." Jill faced the group. "You've done so much for me, I'd like to do something for you. I've asked Gam to bring back a special surprise from Petoskey for all of you. She should be back by now." Jill turned to Sherry. "Would it be all right if I borrow your motor for a few minutes?"

"My motor?" asked Sherry.

"Your wheels, your *car*," said Jill, exasperated.

Sherry was taken aback by the request. "Why don't you ask Gam to bring her surprise here?" she said.

"Gam isn't home. She just dropped things off and kept going."

Sherry said, "We'll have the surprise some other night. Right, you guys?"

Her friends said nothing. They looked at

her stoney eyed, as if she were out to spoil the fun. She felt a twinge but didn't give in.

"Sorry, Jill. Mom and Dad wouldn't like it."

"Mom and Dad," Jill repeated in a broad American accent and everyone laughed, "will never know. I'll be back before the meeting's even adjourned."

"If anything were to happen —" Sherry frowned. "Have you a license?"

"Of course. And I've been driving since I was eleven."

"Eleven? That's illegal around here."

Jill dismissed that. "By the time I took driver's training, I could drive circles round the instructor."

"This conversation is dumb," Sherry said, "because the answer is no."

"What's with you, Sherry?" Kent leaned toward her. "Jill went to a lot of trouble to get us a surprise, and the car and the keys are right here in the barn. It's no big deal."

Sherry wavered. Maybe she was making a flap over nothing. "Are you sure you'll be right back?" She looked Jill squarely in the eye.

"Absolutely, positively." Jill made a dash for the door. "Ten minutes at the most."

Ten minutes passed. Twenty. Forty. Sherry's heart banged against her rib cage as the town hall clock struck the hour.

"I'll have to tell Dad." She shivered.

Just then they heard the sound of a car roaring along Back Road. Everyone held his breath. The car turned in, and Kent ran and swung open the barn door and closed it again. A rush of cold air swept through the barn and the shrill of cicadas echoed in Sherry's ears.

"You're back," Sherry felt both relieved and irritated. "What took you so long?"

"Not to worry." Jill jumped out and lifted a huge sheet cake from the trunk and carried it into the tack room. The overhead light illuminated the king-sized, red frosting letters spelling out BLOCK CLUB, and with smaller letters in pink, FROM JILL, WITH THANKS.

Tina sampled the first slice. "Gorgeous, Jill. There isn't a bakery in Pineridge that could come up to this."

Kent wolfed down a plate-sized slice. "Hope it isn't too soon for seconds."

Sherry nibbled on the sweet cream frosting, and with each bite she felt herself unwind. She did get uptight about too many things.

Everyone stayed later than usual, laughing and talking. Sherry relaxed against Kent's shoulder and when his hand stroked her smooth hair, she settled into a state of calm.

The exodus began at midnight and soon there were just three — Sherry, Kent, and Jill.

"I have to go," Jill said, "and I just wanted to say I'm really sorry about the dent in your father's fender."

Sherry felt the hammer blow to her stomach. "The what?" she said, hoping she hadn't heard.

"It wasn't my doing. Some stupid driver bumped into me, but the police were really hopeless and made it awfully difficult. They just won't accept an English license."

"Oh, Jill . . ." Sherry couldn't go on. It wasn't Jill's fault. Still her parents would be very angry.

Kent inspected the dent with an appraising eye. "We can bump it out," he told Sherry. "Have your father bring it to the garage the first thing tomorrow, and we'll get right at it."

Jill said, "I'm sure Sir will pay for it, but of course it could be weeks or months before the money comes through from Singapore." Enormous eyes gazed at Kent. "You're not angry with me, are you?"

"Of course not. I totaled a car the year I learned to drive, so this little dent is nothing. However, Mr. Russell will not be overjoyed."

A tremor shook Sherry from head to toe. Any time she got out of line, she was grounded or her allowance was stopped — or both. How different it was at the Halliday house with Kent's father trying to make it easy for him ever since his mother died.

"Now, Kent, you know better than that. I don't want to hear about you doing that ever again!" was all Mr. Halliday ever said. And when Kent turned around and broke the rules a second time nothing much happened.

"Sorry about all this, Sherry." Kent leaned back against the hood. "But if you ask me, the best way to handle it is to tell the truth. Again and again you told Jill she could not borrow the family car. But I insisted it was okay for such a short run. Tell your father it was all my fault. I'll take the entire blame."

"Thanks, Kent, but I couldn't do that."

"Not to worry!" Jill spread her hands. "Just say I found the keys and took the car. And if your father says anything to me, he'll be in for it."

FIVE

"Hang on, Sherry!" Jill burst through the wide gym door and leapt down the steps, racing toward the bike rack.

Sherry's fingers tightened on the handlebars as she dragged her feet to a stop.

"You've been avoiding me," Jill said. "Was your father really that ticked-off over a little dent in the fender?"

"It wasn't the dent. It was the fact that I hadn't asked permission for you to use the car."

"Well, you didn't and that's that. I take it the whole bit's blown over by now."

"Not quite."

"Oh?"

Sherry squirmed but it was no use. Jill had cornered her, and she'd have to know sometime.

"I hope you won't be too upset. Dad said

you couldn't come to our house for a month, and I couldn't drive the car for a month."

To Sherry's astonishment, Jill laughed. "Your parents can't be real," she said. "You'd better get them off your back before they muck you up for life." The big, round eyes narrowed. "I suppose Kent's family is up in arms as well."

"Not so you'd notice, but then it wasn't their car." Actually Kent said his father shrugged the incident off with, "Kids will be kids."

"Where is Kent?" Jill zeroed in on Kent's ten-speed bike still in the rack. "I haven't seen him about."

"No one sees him since he made the tennis team. Practice, practice, practice."

"So you're not waiting to meet up with him. Super! Come to our place, where cats are king."

Sherry hesitated. She'd planned to look up F. Scott Fitzgerald at the library.

"Or is my house off limits to you just as yours is off limits to me?" Jill's voice was sharp as a slap.

"Nothing like that," Sherry said hastily.

"Right, then. You'll come. Gam is dying to meet you."

"And I'm dying to meet Gam." Sherry perked up. In spite of Dad's ultimatum, she and Jill could still see each other and be good friends. "I'll phone Mom and tell her where I'm going."

Jill roared. "You mean you have to ask your mummy if you can go home with a friend after school? I gave up that routine with kindergarten."

"It'll only take a sec," Sherry said lightly, knowing full well Mom would send a police search after her if she didn't report in. "There's a phone at Park Pharmacy, and that's right on the way."

"Meet you there." Jill set out on foot.

"Hey!" Sherry said, wheeling her bike to the diagonal walk that led to Main, "where's your bike?"

"Gam wanted to buy me one, but I told her that it wasn't worth it for the short time I'm here."

"We'll take turns," Sherry said. "Ride a block. Walk a block."

Jill shook her head. "Jogging's what I like, but you can take my books." She shoved them in the wicker basket attached to the handlebars and started to run.

Sherry pedaled alongside. Jill's hair was so short there wasn't a hair to fly out of place. Not a bad deal for summer, she decided. To her surprise, Jill speeded up as she went along, moving effortlessly along the tree-lined street. Sherry marveled. Every jogger she knew wore a tortured expression, as if the screws were being tightened with each stride.

"Right there!" Sherry pointed out the pharmacy on the corner of Park and Main.

She kicked down the stand on her bike in front of the window displaying a cardboard blowup of a girl in a bikini with a fiery sunburn: WHY SUFFER? USE SUNSCREEN.

Jill flattened her uptilted nose against the plate glass. "Isn't it a little early for the sunburn season?"

"You don't know Pineridge. Mr. Geezer — honest, that's his real name — put the thing in the window last summer and hasn't gotten around to taking it out yet."

"You're joking!" Jill's hand fluttered to her heart in a feigned attack.

Sherry giggled, then felt a little guilty. "Mr. Geezer really is a fine old gentleman, a friend of my grandfather. He's made up this town's prescriptions for years."

"He looks a bit old," Jill said, peeking through the window.

"He's got young assistants, like his grandson, The Geek. Remember you met him yesterday at lunch? The nice guy with the ears. He's very bright." Sherry rocked forward on the balls of her feet. "Say, you're bright and he's bright; why not haunt the pharmacy on weekends when he works here?"

Jill cocked her head as if listening to an inner voice. "I met all the brains I ever wanted to in London. What I have in mind is something else. One of those big, brawny Americans."

"Oh, there's lots of those around. Take Chip Davis on the football team —"

"I'm off," Jill said before Sherry had a chance to finish her story. "If you don't catch up with me after the phone call, turn right on Laurel Hill Lane, about a mile out of town."

Sherry waved and hurried into the pharmacy.

"Well, if it isn't little Sherry!" Mr. Geezer hobbled over. "What can I do for you today?"

"Just making a call home so Mom will know where I'm going."

He squinted. "Good girl. Things aren't safe like they was fifty years ago, or even yesterday. I've never locked the doors to my house, but now I wonder." He rambled on about the teen punks in ski masks who had robbed the store. "Right here in Pineridge. Can you believe it? They have to be from the city, but why Pineridge?"

"I read about it in the *Bugle*," Sherry nodded sympathetically.

"The sheriff said he has his suspicions, all right, but he told me he'd be in deep trouble if he arrested the wrong boys." Mr. Geezer sucked in his cheeks and it looked as though he was winding up for another long story.

"Excuse me," Sherry said, "but I really do have to call home." Seeing the hurt in his eyes, she added, "But you will tell me all the details the next time I'm in, won't you?"

"Of course. But mind you" — he waggled a finger — "it's not the sort of thing to discuss with just anyone. Some people might get the impression that I can't handle things — the way they pulled a knife on me and made off with the cash register."

"Thankfully you weren't hurt."

Sherry shut herself in the glass booth and dialed.

"Mom," she said, "I'm at Park Pharmacy."

Before she could get another word out, her mother said, "What are you doing there?"

The tone jarred Sherry. Jill was right. Why, at seventeen, must she account for her every move?

"Just reporting in. I'm on my way to Jill's."

"Sherry!" Mom sounded just like the Hatchet Lady. "Your father and I said —"

"You said Jill couldn't come to our house for a whole month. Isn't that cruel enough?"

"I want to go on record as saying that I would prefer that you didn't see Jill at our house or her house, ever. But since you are on your way, there is no point in discussing the matter further." Sherry heard the intake of breath as Mom fought for control. "Get back as soon as you can, dear. And remember, strange cats scratch."

Sherry hung up, wondering why going to Jill's had to cause such a stir. Mounting her bike, she pedaled north on Main, surprised that in the little time she'd been inside, the day had darkened. Bloated clouds hung low on the horizon, and she wondered if the rain that was predicted for tonight might hit sooner.

Laurel Hill Lane wasn't much of a hill, just a sloping street, and if there was any laurel she didn't see it. The gray-shingled house at the end of the lane veered off into several wings, as if the owner couldn't quite make up his mind which room should be added on where.

Jill waited on the low stoop, and Sherry handed her her books. "Lest I forget —"

"Thanks," said Jill. "You took your time."

"Mr. Geezer's long winded."

Jill stepped inside. "Gam!" she shouted.

"Jill-baby!" Gam shouted back as she swept into the hallway.

Sherry tried not to stare, but Gam was unlike any grandmother she'd ever seen. She looked like a blond gypsy, with her dirndl skirt and peasant blouse and gold hoop earrings. She wore outrageous heels and was heavily drenched in some exotic scent.

"This is Sherry," Jill said.

"Sherr-ee, luv," Gam purred. Sherry wondered if she'd picked up the purring sound from living with the cats. "You've made Jill-baby so very happy." She reached out to Jill, and the elastic on the peasant blouse must have been loose, for the blouse fell off her shoulders. "If only I'd had you for a friend at Jill's age, I might not have been so eager to get out of this cage. I might not have eloped with the first boy who came along."

"Oh, then you left here long ago, Mrs. Williams."

"Just call me Gam. And to answer your question, when you're married to a cycle freak you move where the action is: Colorado and the canyons, arenas from coast to coast, over barrels, up walls —"

"You mean he didn't just ride, he jumped?"

"That's the only way he knew how to earn a living." Gam fluffed up her hair, but her lips straightened into a hard line. "Each to his own, I say, but when he found he could make a bundle jumping with my baby on his back, I got out."

Sherry gasped.

"So I raised Jocelyn — that's Jill's mother — with no help from him or anyone else. I've always been proud of that."

The room tilted. What would Mom do if Dad pulled out? One thing for sure. Her own life would be very different. She cleared her throat and asked the question that Mom wanted answered.

"But you came back to Pineridge?"

"Sweetie, when you've done all the things I've had to do, you owe yourself one, and what better place to rest than Pineridge. So let's call my return a gift from me to me — a sabbatical." She took Sherry by the arm, and Sherry caught the glimmer of green nails and rings on each finger. "Come, Sherr-ee, I want you to meet the cat family." Gam opened the screen into the living room.

"You mean they live inside?" Sherry fell back against the screen dumbfounded.

"It's all theirs." Gam beamed.

From inside the door, Sherry scanned the large, sunny room. Seeing is believing, but still . . . Cats perched on the empty bookshelves, on stepladders scattered around the room, on the arms of the overstuffed chairs, on the seats of the straight-backed chairs, on the circular couch in front of the fireplace, and one cat stretched out in the ashes inside the fireplace.

Gam spun around. "And that little room at the back is their dining room." Gam identified the row of bowls on the linoleum and with a ringed finger tested the temperature of the water jetting into the trough. "And the room next door, their bath. They are all toilet trained — Siamese are so much quicker about that sort of thing than the human baby."

Sherry's eyes widened. That explained why the house didn't have that animal-antiseptic smell peculiar to pet shops.

Gam danced over to the palm tree in the huge ceramic pot in the corner of the room. She was really rolling now, like a tour director. "This tree looks like part of the decor, right?" Without waiting for an answer she rushed on. "Actually it's been put here as a scratching post. The young ones are trained to sharpen their claws on the trunk. Unfortunately some of the older ones, set in their ways, sharpen their claws on the trunk only to rip apart the furniture. But since my employer cares deeply for her cats and very little about upholstery —"

"I love cats," Sherry said, "but isn't all this a bit much?"

"Harriet is a lovely lady who has a lot of time and affection to spare for her cat family." Gam stroked a black-masked, blue-eyed Siamese under the chin. The cat made a gargling noise.

"The Siamese are the noisy, demanding ones," Gam explained. "They won't eat this. They won't eat that. But they are favorites of mine." She moved around the room, scratching an ear, brushing the creamy fur with the sharp bristled brush she brought out of her pocket. Hair flew. "This is Ling and that's Lang, her mate. Over there, Chang and Chula. And sitting on the sill, Sirikit. See her long, black-stockinged legs."

Sherry laughed. "Beats me how you can tell them apart."

Gam quirked a jet black brow. "Ah, but they're very different. Ling is the talker. Ming the high jumper. And Chang" — Gam paused by the big cat with a torn ear and one eye — "is boss. He attacks all new cats and brings them in line. But he loves people." Gam tweaked his whiskers. "You can pet him, sweetie."

Sherry reached out, then withdrew her hand. *Strange cats scratch.*

"He won't bite you," Jill said, swinging Chang over her shoulder.

"It isn't that." Sherry puckered up her nose and forced a sneeze. "I guess I'm allergic."

"Oh, dear," Gam said. "Some people are. Maybe you'd better get a breath of air, luv."

"It's been super," Sherry said, closing the screen door behind her.

Jill called out, "Take an antihistamine, Sherry, and come back straight away."

"Thanks," Sherry said, "some other time."

SIX

"Man!" Kent collapsed on the couch in the den. "What a workout. Who says the team is worth it?"

"Of course it is." Sherry tucked a pillow under his head. "Now put your feet up. That's one thing about leather. You can't hurt it."

"Ah, yes." Kent lay back, stretching out his legs — legs that were so long they stretched right over the end of the couch.

Sherry eyed him judiciously. "I can see what you need most is a king-sized bed."

"Come to think of it," Kent said, "we have an old brass bed up in the attic. It belonged to Dad's grandparents. The story goes that Gram and Gramps slept together for forty-eight years, but never spoke a word to each other."

Sherry laughed. "That would never happen to us. We always have so much to say to each other." She held the class ring to the light that was beaming from the table lamp. "Now that I have this, I'm making a hope chest on paper."

"A what?" One brow peaked into a question mark and the other stayed level. Kent could do really tricky things with his eyebrows.

"It sounds crazy," she admitted, "but what with S.A.T.'s and term papers and homework, there's just no time to sit around and feather-stitch a zillion scraps into a quilt, like the ladies of long ago. But I'm clipping and filing like mad. Just yesterday there was the neatest article in the *Bugle* showing an easy way to put shelves together."

Kent cleared his throat. "Before you start building shelves and arranging furniture, don't you think we should decide where this hope chest house is going to be?"

"Pineridge, of course."

"Agreed."

"On the Ridge —"

"Hey! Not so fast. Maybe someday on the Ridge. In the meantime, Dad has other ideas. I'll be getting a beginning mechanic's salary and a bonus every time I bring in someone who buys a car. But we've got to face it. The automobile business isn't the money-maker it once was." His eyes darkened. "And now that Dad has new kids to support, there won't be as much for us."

"We'll work it out." Sherry ran a soothing finger down his cheek. "Remember, the woods behind the barn have been in our family for generations. If Dad let the gang take over the tack room, surely he'll give us some land for our first house." Her eyes sought his. "How about a little cabin in the woods for a starter?"

Kent sprang into a sitting position, his face animated. "I've got it. He snapped his fingers. "The perfect spot. Our Secret Place where we planted the circle of stones as kids."

"Oh, yes." She folded her arms and closed her eyes and pictured the little cabin under the canopy of pine and birch and oak. She would awaken in the morning to the whistle of the cardinal and the caw of the crow and the aroma of coffee brewing. Kent liked his early-morning coffee and so did she.

"Let's go!" Kent jumped up.

"Are you out of your mind? That rain isn't rain anymore. It's a deluge."

Rain rat-a-tatted on the flat roof and slurped down the drain pipes. She had no intention of leaving the cozy room with the drawn drapes and mellow light for a soaking.

"What's a little rain —"

"Forget it. You know what the path is like in the rain. Mud-gluck. Besides, I just finished drying my hair." She looked at him carefully, trying to read any change in expression. "I'm thinking of cutting it off for the summer."

"You'll do no such thing!" Kent's vehemence surprised her.

"Suddenly you're the great macho hero!"

she teased. But she was glad to hear that Kent liked her long hair as much as she did.

Kent took a step toward her. "You bet," he said, and laughed. He buried his head in the nape of her neck. He lifted her chin and found her lips. He held her so close that she forced herself to back off.

"Hey, Kent, you came over to study." She tried a no-nonsense approach but her voice faltered. "We haven't cracked a book."

"Who cares?"

"Please," she begged, "I feel just like you do, but someday we'll have a wedding no one will ever forget. We'll exchange rings and have all our friends in the Block Club for bridesmaids and ushers and a cake a mile high and a honeymoon on the beach of Waikiki."

"And when is all this taking place?"

"Sooner than you think." She clasped her hands around the ring. "I always thought I wanted to go on to college, and Miss Hatcher and Mom and Dad keep bugging me. But college isn't where my heart is."

"That's what I've been waiting to hear." Kent wrapped his hands around her hands that held the ring. "Why sweat all that useless information when we could be together in our very own cabin in the woods?"

"Oh, Kent, you know it's not useless information," Sherry said quickly. "But a cabin in the woods . . ." She repeated the words, and they sounded golden.

The phone rang, snapping her out of her dream.

"Hello," she said, feeling a touch resentful at the interruption. But hearing Jill's voice, she rallied. "Oh, hi, Jill. Sorry I had to rush away from your place today," she said. "I just loved meeting Gam and the cat family. A real circus." But when Jill told her that she'd left her French book in the front hall, Sherry caught her breath. "I must have handed it to you along with your books. Even if Madame Joneau flunks me, there's no way I'm going out in this rain." She paused. "No, no!" Sherry protested, "don't even think of bringing it over. I can live without it. Hello! Hello!" She turned to Kent. "Jill hung up on me. You don't suppose she's making Gam drive her over in this monsoon?"

"Hardly. You told her not to." Kent's face took on a quizzical expression. "You didn't tell me you'd been with Jill today."

"We were too busy talking about us." Sherry sat down on the couch. The thunder seemed louder and the rain slip-slapped on the window panes. She sighed. "It's a lousy deal, but you know Jill isn't welcome here, so when she asked me back to her place, I felt the least I could do was to go. And I wouldn't have missed it for anything." She plumped up the cushion alongside her. "Sit here, and I'll tell you all about it."

Once he was settled she told him about the scratching tree and the cats' dinette and bath. The way Kent looked she was sure he thought she was putting him on, but the funny part was that it was true.

"Can you imagine turning the best room in the house over to a cat family?" she asked.

"The lady has to be nuts."

"The boss cat is mean but the others are real dolls. Especially Ming. She's such a lady the way she holds her head and lifts her paws. I would just love a little Siamese kitten with big blue eyes."

"What good would a kitten do you when you're alone in the woods all day?"

"Oh, Kent, I'd love a little cat as a pet."

"What you need is a guard dog, a German shepherd or a Doberman."

She shuddered. "I'd be too scared of a Doberman."

Kent put his hand on her shoulder. "You want to feel safe when you're alone, don't you?"

"Pineridge is the safest place in the entire state. The *Bugle* just ran the statistics proving it."

"The *Bugle* also ran a story about the robbery at the Park Pharmacy. The robbers, as far as I know, are still on the loose."

"One isolated case —" Sherry drew in her breath. What had happened? A moment ago she and Kent had been making beautiful music, sharing plans for their wedding, sharing plans for a dream cabin in the woods, and now they were almost fighting.

"Come on, Kent," she said tenderly, "it's getting late and we have a civics quiz to prepare for."

Kent yawned. "If you ask me, the whole judicial system is a bore."

"Mr. Mason is positively enamored of the courts." Sherry flipped through the civics books. "Start here, chapter fifteen. All Mason's favorite theories are underlined in red."

"What would I ever do without you?" Kent said.

"You'll never have to." She touched the ring. *Always.*

Kent moved over to the far corner of the couch, and she looked at him with a sidelong glance, glad to see that he was concentrating. She tackled her math. She liked math. If you did it logically, it always came out right.

Suddenly they heard a pounding on the front door. Sherry jumped. "Who'd want to be out in all this rain?"

"Some idiot," Kent said.

"Hope it's no emergency." She pictured the frail and ancient Mrs. Brophy living alone next door.

"I'll get it," Kent said.

Watching Kent stride through the living room and disappear around the corner into the hall, Sherry felt bad vibes all around her. Should she call Dad? The front door creaked open. A low whistle as only Kent could whistle, and with a thumping heart she leapt up and raced toward the door.

In the hall she stopped abruptly, as if nailed to the floor. Jill stood on the threshold in a warm-up suit, dripping water from head to toe.

"The French book," she said cheerfully, holding out a plastic bag. "Believe me, you'll need it. Madame Joneau is out for blood."

"Thanks," Sherry said, adding, "Come in." For the moment her innate sense of hospitality overcame her shock, and she was too flustered to remember that Jill was off limits for another three weeks.

"Don't mind if I do," Jill said, swimming over the threshold.

SEVEN

Sherry's eyes flicked from Jill to the staircase and back again. No sign of Mom and Dad yet. But suppose they came out of their room and found Jill standing in the hall. And to make matters worse, the pool of water at her feet was oozing across the Oriental runner onto the hand-rubbed oak floor that Mom treated with TLC. She had to get Jill out of here, fast.

She put a finger to her lips and backoned, leading the way along the corridor, relieved to hear the waves of dubbed-in laughter exploding in the master bedroom above. She moved faster past the dining room and reaching the kitchen door, held it open for Jill and Kent. Once they were safely inside, she sagged back, exhaling in long, noisy gasps.

"Whew! We made it!"

"Made what?" Jill bent over the sink, squeezing water out of her sweat shirt.

"Made the kitchen. I told you that you couldn't come here until the month is up."

Jill looked puzzled. "You mean that your parents wouldn't even let you ask me inside in all this rain?"

"They'd have my scalp."

"Worry not," Jill said with a lift of her chin. "I wouldn't dream of getting you in trouble. I'm off for home."

"Not in this downpour, you're not," Kent said.

"Who knows?" Jill shrugged. "Maybe it'll rain forty days and forty nights. I might as well go now."

Kent leaned against the counter. "Oh, Jill, maybe if you wait a little while, the rain will let up."

Sherry glanced at the kitchen clock.

"You know how it goes, Kent. Twenty-five minutes from now, Dad'll clomp down the stairs and flash the hall lights off and on and say, 'Good night, Kent' and he'll expect the usual, 'I was just leaving, Mr. Russell.'"

"Really?" Jill rubbed her head round and round with a kitchen towel. "How can a guy look so nice and be such a menace?"

Sherry clenched her teeth. Jill had it all wrong. Dad was the best dad ever. She appealed to Kent.

"Let's just say we have to come up with a game plan. Rain or no rain, Jill has to be out of here in twenty-five — oops — twenty-four minutes."

"In the meantime," Kent said, "how about a snack?"

Sherry smiled indulgently. Kent was forever hungry. When they were married, it would only make sense to plant a vegetable garden and to keep a cow.

"Well, I can tell you this much. There's no time for a pizza. You know where the cookies are, and if you want a Coke try the bottom shelf of the fridge."

"And bring one for me, Kent," Jill said, dumping the water out of her running shoes down the drain. "I won't be a minute."

Sherry sat down opposite Kent at the breakfast room table and kept her eyes on the clock. With each circle of the second hand, she felt her chest constrict. The weather was worsening. Zigzags of lightning forked across the sky. Rain pinged like shots from a BB gun on the roof. She lifted her glass to her lips but her lips trembled, and she put the glass down.

"There, now," Jill sighed contentedly as she slipped into the seat alongside Kent. "I'm okay. You okay?"

Kent laughed.

"If you'll just pass the cookies, Kent —"

Sherry's head began to spin. She shook it, trying to sort out the sequence of events that led to this moment.

Jill nibbled on a cookie and sipped her Coke as if she had all the time in the world.

"Did you hear the one about the Hatchet Lady and the jar of jelly beans?" She started to giggle before she even began to tell the joke.

Sherry clamped her hands over her ears. Like another time, another place. Her mind ran off an instant replay of the day she'd been called into the office, working herself into a lather, while Jill, who was the cause of the summons, dozed placidly in the office chair.

Sherry waited for Kent's laughter to subside. "What I can't understand," she said leaning across the table, "is how Gam would let you out on a night like this."

"Gam doesn't know," Jill said. When Sherry gulped, Jill reassured her. "Oh, I left her a note. I wouldn't want Gam to worry. But chances are I'll be home before she gets back."

Sherry nodded. "I see. She had to go out. That's why she couldn't drive you."

"She's gone to the Hideaway. She says she gets tired of conversing with cats all day, and she needs people-talk for a change."

"But the Hideaway!" Sherry straightened. Mom had told her all about the disco on the edge of town, and Sherry had gotten the impression that it wasn't a very pleasant place.

Now it was Jill who leaned across the table, flecks of anger sharpening her eyes.

"And what's the matter with the Hideaway?"

Sherry felt her face redden, but she tried to answer honestly. "I've never been there but Mom said it's a meeting place for singles."

"Well, Gam is single."

"I mean *young* singles."

"That suits Gam. She likes young people."

Sherry felt the pain in back of her eyes, and Jill swam out of focus.

"As a matter of fact," Jill said cheerfully, "the last time Gam went there she got in with the bouncer. Gam always says a girl's best friend is the bouncer."

Sherry concentrated on the clock.

"Look," she told Jill as the second hand circled again, "I hate sending you out in all this rain . . ."

"What's a little pneumonia between friends?" Jill chirruped. She stood up and stretched. Actually she looked quite revived, rosy lipped and rosy cheeked. She started for the back door, only managing a few steps before lightning illuminated the room in a blinding flash and thunder shook the window-panes. Ozone laced the air. For a brief instant, everyone stopped, stunned. Jill was the first to recover.

"Close." She waved. "Wish me luck!"

Kent wheeled on Sherry. "You aren't going to let her go out in this?"

Sherry grasped the edge of the table. "And what do you suggest?"

"I'll swipe Dad's car keys and drive her home."

"Okay," Sherry said, "that one's on you."

"I don't know what's come over you," Kent said. "You've always been so understand-ing —"

"Go!" Sherry cried out as she heard the grandfather clock in the hall gong the hour.

Without a backward glance, Kent took Jill by the elbow and slammed out the garden door.

"Cheers!" Jill called over her shoulder.

Sherry began to shake. But she had to keep going. She grabbed Jill's glass and washed it and returned it to the shelf. Tucking a roll of paper towels under her arm, she rushed down the hall to the front of the house. She dropped to her knees and began mopping up the pool of water on the waxed floor just as Dad started down the stairs.

"What's all this?" Dad towered over her. Out of the corner of her eye she saw the pin-striped pant legs, the polished shoes. She wanted desperately to confide in him and ask his forgiveness in admitting Jill. But how could she? He would never understand about the French book and letting Jill in on such a flimsy excuse.

"An accident," she said. "I spilled a glass of water."

"Now, Sherry," Dad said fondly, "you never spill anything. And you don't need to cover for Kent. We all know he's a bull in a china shop." He looked around. "Where is Kent? The least he could do is mop it up himself."

"I sent him home." Sherry felt guilty. She had never lied to Dad. But it wasn't exactly a lie. "That last crash of thunder did it."

Dad nodded. "I wouldn't be at all surprised if lightning struck one of the big trees."

Sherry bunched up the wet towels. The woods. The dream cabin. She felt a sense of despair. How could she talk over the plans for the cabin with Dad when at this very moment Kent was driving Jill home and she was on her knees trying to repair the damage Jill had done to the oak floor?

EIGHT

Madame Joneau waited inside the classroom door, a set smile on her lips, carrying on with the ritual she'd started the first day of school last fall.

"Bonjour, Mademoiselle Sherr-ee."

"Bonjour, Madame Joneau." Sherry tried not to look shocked. Such a short time ago Madame had been plump as a pastry, but now she was as thin and brittle as a strand of raw spaghetti. Her watch dangled from her bony wrist, and her skirt cinched in by a wide, patent belt was too long and too loose. And no ring.

Moving toward the back of the room, out from under Madame's sharp eye, Sherry wondered about the ring. Had she left it home so it wouldn't slip off her skinny finger, or was this her way of telling the world that she and Mr. Jones had split?

Sherry touched her own ring, remembering the night Kent had given it to her, and how he had said there had always been just the two of them and that's the way it always would be.

Where was Kent? She had to talk to him. From the moment she'd arrived at school this morning, she'd been on the lookout for him, but he wasn't at his usual hangouts, his locker, or the tennis court. At lunch she'd glimpsed a tall boy across the cafeteria, but the boy did a disappearing act before she reached the checkout counter.

Sitting down by the half-open window she felt the cool breeze on her cheek and caught the pungent after-rain smell of damp earth, wet grass clippings, and drenched lilac. Today Pine Creek would be overflowing. Had Kent gone fishing? She sketched a round fish-eye on her scratch pad. No, she decided Kent had not gone fishing. Truancy was the one thing Miss Hatcher never forgave. Kent had gone that route once, and he wasn't likely to put himself in that bind again — especially now that he'd made the tennis team.

Little threads of worry tangled in her mind. Was Kent sick? Last night he'd arrived in the rain. When he'd left the rain was really bucketing down. He'd looked healthy enough, but viruses had struck down more than one giant.

"Okay if I sit here?" Sherry blinked. The

Geek — Mr. Geezer's grandson. A nice enough guy, but she had expected Kent.

"Sure," she said. How could she hold a seat for Kent when she had no idea if he was even in school?

"Have you seen Kent around?" she asked.

"No, but that doesn't mean much. We don't take the same things."

Sherry turned to face the door. Madame Joneau was doing her greeting thing with the twins with the flower names, Lily and Iris. Lily was wearing a white ribbon in her hair, Iris a purple ribbon. Really corny. Now Jill! Sherry stiffened. Jill breezed by Madame Joneau, and spotting Sherry smiled and waved, apparently unaware of the commotion her surprise visit had caused.

Sherry made a show of talking to The Geek. She had no intention of conversing with Jill until she'd heard Kent's version of last night's happening. Out of the corner of her eye, Sherry watched Jill sit down front row center and was relieved that she wasn't trying to muscle into a seat alongside her.

The Geek leaned closer. "Guess who came in when I was working at the pharmacy last night?"

"I wouldn't know."

"Madame Joneau," The Geek said in a conspiratorial whisper. "Grandpa filled a prescription for tranquilizers Doc had ordered for her."

"She sure needs them. She looks ready to jump out of her skin."

The buzzer sounded and Madame Joneau reached for the door. Just as she was closing it, Kent slipped through, folding his lanky torso into the first vacant seat. Madame Joneau glared, and Sherry knew he was in for it. She could see Kent wasn't dying or anything, but he didn't look like himself either, with his head hanging and a troubled expression clouding his eyes.

Madame Joneau tapped her pointer on the desk and launched into roll call.

"Mary Anne Abbot."

A hand shot up. "*Ici.*"

"Elizabeth Becker."

Sherry concentrated on the back of Kent's head. The hair was longer than usual and curlier, too, camouflaging the classic shape of his head. But if Kent's hair was a little long, The Geek's was too short to hide his stick-out ears. Not that his ears bothered him.

"Me and Prince Charles," he always said.

"Kent Halliday," Madame Joneau snapped.

No response. If only he had come earlier he would have been seated at her side and she could have alerted him, but as it was he was on his own.

"*Kent Halliday!*" The voice shrilled with exasperation.

Kent's chin jerked up. "Here. I mean *ici.*"

"We are happy you've seen fit to return from outer space, and if it isn't asking the impossible we would appreciate your giving us your full attention for the remainder of the period."

"Yes, ma'am. Sorry. Madame."

Sherry gave The Geek a look. *Is she ever in a foul mood*, it said.

"Iris Hunt," Madame Joneau continued, and now her voice softened. Iris was her favorite, always prepared, and as fascinated by every facet of France as Madame was. It was Iris who brought in the pictures of famous Frenchmen and posted them around the room. The funny thing was that the most famous "Frenchman" of all was a woman, Madame Curie, and Polish at that, even if France claimed her for her own.

"Jill Keller," Madame Joneau said.

"Ici." Jill answered promptly, and Kent looked at Jill for a long minute, then hunkered down in his chair. What was he thinking? Was he worrying about leaving with Jill last night? Was he worrying about the French lesson? But what did it matter? Even if she hadn't left her French book at Jill's, she and Kent had been in no mood last night to work on the translation. They had been making plans for their future. She could see it all now, the cabin nestled among the tall pines, the twilight sun sifting through the needled branches.

Madame Joneau shut the roll book. "Now turn to page seventy-eight. Who would like to translate?"

Iris waved both hands. Wouldn't she just!

Iris and Lily might look like Xerox copies of each other, but Iris was forever jumping up like a jack-in-the-box and Lily was as timid as a dormouse.

Madame Joneau ignored the waving hands and pointed at Kent.

"Now if you'll begin with the second paragraph. Read the French, then translate."

Kent gulped. "Yep. I mean *oui*. Now let's see. Do you call that place the *Champs Elysée*?"

"Non! Non!" Madame Joneau rolled her eyes and clapped her hands over her ears. "We do not say *champs* like boxing champs. The word begins with a 'shh' sound. Like this." She puckered up her lips and intoned the sentence in a lilting voice.

Sherry could have died for Kent, but then who said a mechanic needed French? It was different for Madame Joneau, whose happiness was making music out of French words.

Jill rose up from her front row seat. She stood with her feet firmly planted on the floor, hands on hips.

"You may be seated," Madame Joneau said.

"Not until I tell you what I think of your accent," Jill said coolly.

"Sit down," Madame Joneau took a step toward Jill.

Jill did not budge. "Hear this! *Votre accent est si mauvais que si vous allez à Paris personne ne vous comprendrait.*"

She spoke so slowly and distinctly that Sherry had no trouble translating the insult:

78

"Your accent is so bad that if you went to Paris no one would understand you."

Madame Joneau's face went scarlet and then slowly blanched into paste.

"Get out! Get out!" Her hands began to shake. "Take this slip to Miss Hatcher's office, and do not come back."

"As you wish." Jill shrugged, and walked toward the door. At the door she turned and saluted the tri-color French flag in its stand in the corner.

The class suppressed giggles, and Madame Joneau gasped as she sank down in the chair behind the desk. She rummaged through a drawer and brought out a compact, but the makeup mirror could not conceal the tears brimming over her lids and spilling down her cheeks.

"Serves her right," The Geek said.

"Yeah," Sherry said, but suddenly she was sad. How did it feel to split up from the man you once loved and then be shafted by one of your students? In no time at all Madame Joneau would be the laughingstock of Pineridge High.

"Iris" — Madame Joneau waved a hand — "translate."

That was her last word for the rest of the period. Iris concluded the translation, and when she sat down Madame Joneau wrote the next assignment on the board with the notation, "If you do not understand come to the desk."

The room settled into an eerie quiet. In

study hall there was always an undercurrent of whispering, but now there was no sound except an occasional cough that seemed overly loud and the squeak of a chair. The bell rang at last, and everyone filed out. It was like a funeral procession, and Sherry knew that Madame Joneau had taken Jill's insult far too much to heart.

NINE

Sherry broke into a run, zigzagging through the crowded hall until she caught up with Kent.

"My God," he said, "what do you suppose will happen to her?"

"I feel so bad for her," Sherry said. "Once the story gets around, she'll be the joke of the whole school and that's rough."

"What do you mean — joke? She's a hero showing up that French phony."

Sherry stared. "Who are we talking about?"

"Who do you think? Jill, of course. Right this minute she's locked up in the Hatchet House, and who knows what the Hatchet Lady is doing to her."

Sherry's head jerked. In her concern for Madame Joneau, she'd quite forgotten Jill.

"Save your sympathy," Sherry said coldly. "Even the Hatchet Lady will find her hard to handle."

"You don't understand." Anger smouldered in Kent's eyes. "She's being punished because of *me*. She was trying to rescue me. She knew I hadn't done my homework."

Sherry gasped. "How could she know that?"

"On the way home I told her, and she said that if Madame Joneau picked on me she'd fix Madame Joneau."

Sherry stepped in front of Kent blocking his path. "You mean to tell me that the scene was all arranged?"

"Certainly not," Kent said, striding ahead again. "The last thing I wanted was to be late to that class, but some guy got my racquet by mistake and I had to chase him down."

The taut muscles in Sherry's throat relaxed a little. So it wasn't something the two of them had cooked up together! Kent was a victim of circumstance.

He started up the back stairs and Sherry hurried to keep abreast of him. "Now about last night," she said, "how did things go with you?"

"About what you'd expect. We were practically drowned by the time we reached my house. Dad was still up, and I asked him if I could take the car and drive Jill home and he wanted to know what I was doing walking around in the rain with her."

"Wasn't he fit to be tied?"

"Why should he be?"

"You know. At my place there'd be a court-martial."

82

"Oh, I told him Jill had been visiting you but you couldn't use the car, and your parents were ready for bed so I offered. Hope you don't mind if I told a little white lie on your behalf."

Sherry's lips twisted. "Not at all. I had to tell a little white lie on your behalf. Remember the puddle Jill made in the front hall? Dad was curious and I couldn't very well say Jill had made the mess, so when he figured that you were the culprit, I let it go. He wanted to know why you hadn't stayed to mop it up, but I said I'd made you leave because of the storm." Sherry looked at Kent. "Sure hope we don't have to go on this way — telling one lie after the other all because of Jill."

Kent stopped abruptly. "How come you're following me up the back stairs? You don't take shop."

Sherry reached for the rail, hanging on to it as if it were a lifeline. "I know I'm going the wrong way. But I didn't see you all morning and I wanted to know what happened last night." She straightened and her voice edged. "Besides, you don't need to snap at me, Kent."

"Sorry. I didn't mean to — honest." He dropped his head again, an ungainly gesture that disconcerted her. He fumbled with his books and looked down. "I don't know what's bit me," he said.

TEN

"What do you think, Sherry?" Tina twirled in front of the triple mirror in Glory-Bee's dress shop. "The truth, even if it hurts."

"I like it," Sherry said.

"If that's all you can give it —"

"I like the fit and the swingy skirt. Only —"

"Only what?" Tina's eyes narrowed behind her long lashes.

"Well, with your gorgeous black hair, I'd like to see you in white."

"White is out," Tina said emphatically. "This is for a prom, not my wedding."

"But you and Brian will be leading the grand march. You need something sensational. As a matter of fact," Sherry said as she helped Tina out of the gown, "there's a hot pink number on the rack."

"Yeah, I walked right to it yesterday. Size five. I'd need two of them."

"Oh Tina, don't be silly. Anyway, what's the hurry?" Sherry said. "The prom's a month away. Try Marshall's. If they don't have it on the floor, you can always order from their catalogue."

"And look like everyone else?"

"You could never look like anyone else."

"Well, it's an idea. Maybe Ms. G.B. can order this blue in torchy orange or lurid lavender."

"I'll try," Ms. G.B. promised. She jotted down Tina's phone number. "And I'm getting in a new shipment of prom dresses any day now. So do come back." She flashed Sherry a smile. "I'm sure there'll be something for you, dear."

"Thanks," Sherry said knowing that it was futile. Mom was acting really chintzy, dredging up all those old bromides. *Waste not, want not,* she had said, insisting that Sherry wear the bridesmaid's dress that she'd worn last August at her cousin's wedding in Kalamazoo and had never had on again. Not that she ever wanted to.

"It's very becoming," Mom had said.

"I feel like a baby in it."

"Nonsense. If you don't like the scoop neck, I'll square it off for you. And it shouldn't be any trouble at all removing the cap sleeves, if that's the problem, although personally I think the gown is lovely just the way it is."

Sherry gravitated to the mannequin in skinny black with the plunging neckline and spaghetti straps. Not for her, but if Ms. G.B. got in something fantastic, she just might dip into her savings and treat herself to a new gown. Dad would disapprove, of course. Bankers really had their value system all messed up. If it was fun, it had to be wrong.

"Savings are for emergencies," Dad always said, and Sherry was certain that anything as frivolous as a dance wouldn't qualify for a withdrawal.

"C'mon, Sherry," Tina said, "we've seen it for now. Maybe next week we'll luck out."

An ugly thought planted itself in Sherry's mind. Mom and Tina both took it for granted that she was going to the prom with Kent, but Kent had never mentioned it. Her hand flew to her ring. She was getting paranoid. Of course they would be going together. Hadn't they always?

"Now that you've delivered me from a baby blue prom," Tina said, "we'll get your favorite flavor at Benno's and then go to the park."

"I shouldn't." Sherry stood uncertainly on the curb watching the light turn from red to green and back again. "My report on *The Great Gatsby* is long overdue and I haven't started on my history term paper and Monday there's a math quiz." She rocked back on her heels. "I don't need a treat. I've got to study."

"Forget it," Tina said. "I've had my eye on you. You're all uptight. Believe me, you'll do better if you relax a bit."

Was Tina right? She had gone to the library all yesterday afternoon, and when Kent couldn't come over last night she had locked herself in her room to study, but had accomplished nothing — unless two sentences of a term paper could be called an accomplishment.

"Let's go!" Tina started to run when the light turned green again.

Benno's was the narrow building squeezed between Marshall's department store and Kresge's. It was a one-man operation with a counter and carry-out service.

"I'm not the least hungry," Sherry said, settling on a spun sugar cone that was a mile high. The pink froth melted instantly at the touch of her tongue.

"I'll never forget my first encounter with one of these," Sherry said as she ambled along Main. "Dad said circuses didn't come all that often to Pineridge, and he took me out of kindergarten to go. We were early and he bought me a spun sugar cone. Well, an elephant trumpeted behind me and I dropped the cone and it slid all the way down the front of me. I was so sticky Dad gave me a bath in the drinking fountain."

"Yup." Tina took a lick of her caramel nut concoction. "Isn't it funny the way we remember the dumb things? Like the first time I went to Sunday school I took a dime out of the plate instead of putting one in."

Sherry laughed, and it occurred to her that

she had laughed very little in the past couple of weeks.

"Let's find a bench in the sun," Tina announced as they walked through the gateway of Pineridge Park.

"I'm all for that," Sherry said, thinking how much better summer things looked with a tan.

The park opened officially on Memorial Day when the fountain was turned on, the flag run up, and a band played. Right now there were only a few kids on skateboards and one old man bundled up in a greatcoat and scarf with a felt hat pulled down over his ears. He looked at them over the rim of his ragged newspaper.

Sherry whispered, "Hasn't anyone told him it's spring?"

"That's what comes from reading old newspapers," Tina said.

Sherry groaned.

"Right here, Sherry. A whole row of benches just for us."

"Isn't it fun having the place all to ourselves?" Sherry rolled up her pants legs and sat down, stretching her legs the length of the bench. May. The lilacs were fading, but the flowering crabs were in burgundy bloom and the black-limbed Judas tree was aglow with reddish purple blossoms.

"Once I wrote a poem called 'Purple Paradise.'"

"How awful," Tina said.

"It really was. But the thing is I could pour

it all out. The night Kent gave me his ring I wrote seventeen poems. Now I have writer's block, and I don't know what to do about it."

"Writer's block," Tina said, "is like insomnia. The more you worry about it, the worse it gets."

"What do you suggest?"

"I suggest you get your mind on my problems." Tina ransacked her canvas tote and brought out a small spiral notebook. "P is for potluck," she thumbed through the pages. "It's coming up fast. Can I count on you for a casserole?"

"You bet."

"I'm glad everyone isn't like Midge who'll just bring pickles or Tubby with his offer of paper napkins."

Sherry tilted her face into the sun. She closed her eyes, but instead of a blackout, her eyelids shimmered with red velvet.

"What have you in mind?" She asked with a yawn.

"Well, your super-duper chicken went big last year. Not a bite left. Kent had three helpings."

Kent. She knew he loved her chicken casserole. But why should she skin all that chicken for someone who had barked at her? He'd said he was sorry, but he wasn't acting all that contrite.

"Maybe I'll do my easy Stroganoff," she said.

Either Tina didn't hear or chose not to. "Well, that's settled," she announced, and wrote sup-dup-chic opposite Sherry's name. "Everyone's coming," Tina added. "That makes thirteen. Remember how Midge tried to use that silly superstition to keep Jill out? Thank heavens you wouldn't buy it. And I kept looking for a bylaw to sidetrack her, but the truth is there are several deadbeats in the Club, and Jill more than carries her own weight."

"Meaning what?" Sherry swung her legs around and sat up very straight against the hard-backed bench.

"She's not only bringing a main dish but she offered to do all the decorations."

"We've never bothered with decorations before," Sherry said.

"That's just it! Decorations add something and so long as she's willing to go to all that trouble —"

Suddenly Sherry felt chilled. She wrapped her arms around herself, wishing she were bundled up like the old man near the gate.

"Jill can bear watching," she said.

Tina turned. "What brought that on?"

Tina was her best friend. They had always confided in each other and more than ever she needed a confidante. If ever there was a time and a place. . .

"You won't believe this." Sherry proceeded to give a blow-by-blow recital of the ill-fated night when Jill arrived with the French book in the rain. "There she was dripping water all over the front hall when she knew that she wasn't allowed on our property. I hid her in the kitchen and just when the storm was really raging I had to shoo her out the back door."

"So she jogged home in the rain?"

"No," Sherry said with a touch of asperity, "Kent got in the act and drove her."

Tina laughed. "Sounds like a soap opera."

Sherry tried to laugh, too, but the laugh turned sour. "I have a feeling I didn't handle things right." She brushed a maple spinner off her lap and ground the seed under her heel. "Suppose this happened to you, Tina? What would you have done?"

"It never would have happened at our house," Tina said. "That bratty sister of mine would have been at the door before the bell stopped ringing and she would have squealed to Father, who would have taken care of things right away."

"Maybe that's what I should have done. Called Dad."

"Hey, you're a big girl, and you did just what I would have done under the circumstances. Invite Jill in and hope the rain would stop. Well, it didn't. And Kent came to the rescue, so what's bugging you?"

"Well, that was Wednesday night. And the very next day, Jill pulled the rug out from under Madame Joneau."

"Now, Sherry, you know the way Madame has been carrying on the past few weeks. She was asking for it."

"What's happened to her? We have a sub day after day, and no one ever mentions Madame Joneau at all."

"Don't quote me, but the rumor is that Madame went home that night and collapsed. A neighbor happened by and rushed her to emergency. Now she's on sick leave."

"How do you like that?" Sherry said bitterly. "Jill driving her right over the brink."

"Wait a minute!" Tina cleared her throat. "You can't lay that on Jill."

"Let's just say Jill did what she could to make a bad situation worse. Harassing someone who's already upset is like kicking a man when he's down." Sherry felt anger roil up inside her like molten lava. "And, frankly, I don't know why Miss Hatcher didn't suspend Jill once and for all. She's getting off easy. Detention every day after school isn't all that bad, but Kent is so dense he thinks the poor little thing is being abused."

Tina looked amused. "Jealous, eh?"

"Certainly not!" Sherry shouted. Tina backed off. In that instant Sherry became painfully aware of her loud, irate voice.

"Sorry, Tina," she said, forcing a smile. "I don't know what's bit me."

It was only after the words were out that she realized that those were the exact same words Kent had said to her.

ELEVEN

"Why, Mrs. Brophy," Sherry paused under the beech tree as she met up with her next-door neighbor on Back Road. "I didn't know you had a dog."

"How could you, my dear? I just got him."

The miniature poodle danced around Sherry's feet, haranguing her in short, staccato barks.

"He's adorable. I'd pet him except for this —" She regripped the handles on the casserole. "Tina's having the Block Club potluck supper tonight."

"It smells delicious." Mrs. Brophy said, and when the puppy stood on his hind legs wriggling his black rubbery nose, she added, "Joey thinks so, too."

"Joey must like chicken."

"Joey likes anything. But don't let me keep you." Mrs. Brophy waved Sherry on, and Sherry thought what a nice old lady she was.

"Actually I'm early." Secretly she was hoping that Kent would look out his window and catch up with her.

"Sit, Joey, sit," Mrs. Brophy commanded, but Joey strained at the leash, panting after a squirrel chittering up a tree.

"You're something taking on a puppy," Sherry said. "Mom says puppies are a lot of work."

"My son insisted."

"Your son?"

"But, of course, you've never met him. He moved to California before you were born and only returns every few years. He says it's easier for me to visit him than for his big family to visit me, although as you know I have room for all." She lowered her voice as if someone were listening, even though they were all alone. "The fact is he feels deprived without his golf course and his swimming pool."

"But we have a golf course — Pineridge Municipal."

"He said he'd rather be stuck in the gorse in Scotland than fight his way out of that uncouth, unkempt, uncut — those are his words, mind you — municipal course. He's trying to persuade me to move to California, but I had the last word. I told him I was too old for the bikini culture."

"You're not too old for anything." Sherry smiled.

"Oh, that's the nicest thing a pretty young girl could possibly say! But he does worry about my living alone, and he made me promise to get a dog. Of course he thinks it's a standard poodle, but I don't want anything around bigger than I am." She tapped her shoe. "Sit, Joey, *sit*." She sighed. "As you can see, he's got the better of me already."

Joey's tail wagged faster and faster.

"He's awfully cute," Sherry said. "But a watch dog?"

Mrs. Brophy picked Joey up, and the pink tongue licked her ear under the cloud of white hair.

"If you ever get stuck for someone to walk him," Sherry said, "I'd be glad to."

"No wonder I've never wanted to leave Pineridge! Where else would I ever get an offer like that?"

Sherry smiled. It had been a while since she'd had such a good feeling inside. She glanced down the road behind her. Still empty.

"Have you seen Kent around?" she asked.

"From the looks of the Halliday lawn, I'd say he hasn't been around at all."

TWELVE

The stockade fence ended. The iron fence with spearpoints began. Behind the iron fence and across the rise of lawn, the Trowbridge mansion with its turrets and towers, high brick chimneys, and cupola dominated the Ridge.

How much longer will it survive? Sherry asked herself, as she did every time she pulled the latch on the gate and walked across the overgrown flagstone path leading to the front entrance. The Pineridge Historical Society had declared the mansion an historical landmark, but the townspeople called it the "mad monstrosity" and wouldn't contribute a dime toward its preservation.

"If it ever goes on the market," Midge's father said with regret, "we could never find a buyer to take it on."

For Sherry it was neither a landmark nor a monstrosity. It was a house of happy memories. They had played hide-and-seek in the turrets, raced up the front stairs and down the back, and spooked each other in the dungeonlike cellars.

"We have a dinosaur on our hands," Tina had confided to Sherry the year they'd let the gardener and housekeeper go and turned the thermostat down to fifty-eight degrees. "The only way we can keep the house we love is to shrink it down to size."

First to be sealed off were the turrets and cellars, then all the extra bedrooms and the back halls and the servants' quarters. Now the Trowbridges were reduced to living in the front parlor, the kitchen, and the upstairs family suite. The great dining hall and the one-time sumptuous living room were opened only for special occasions — the annual pot-luck being one of them.

Now, as Sherry made her way up the porch steps, she noticed new signs of decay in the fretwork along the eaves and despaired. She rang the bell, answered instantly by Tina's younger sister Caroline, alias Chippie. With her usual lack of diplomacy, Chippie blurted out, "Where's Kent?"

"His tennis match must be taking forever," Sherry said sweetly.

"Are you sure it's tennis?" said Chippie, coyly.

"I really must get the chicken in the oven," Sherry stepped past her into the hall. Poor Tina! What had she done to deserve someone so gross for a sister? She passed through the familiar corridor, with its dark wood paneling and fireplace at the far end, which was ornately tiled and surmounted by a half-moon gilt mirror.

"Sherry!" Tina ran the length of the living room. "I don't know what I would have done without you yesterday. As it is, I worked most of the night."

"T'was fun," Sherry said wondering why she found cleaning her own room such a drag when a really big job like opening up a living room that had been closed off for the winter was a challenge.

"I never want to see another dustcover," Tina said. "All that collection of dust ended up in my hair."

"It looks divine."

"Three shampoos later."

"Am I first?"

"Jill arrived some time ago and locked herself in the dining room and won't let anyone in, which is fine with me." Tina reached for the casserole that Sherry was holding. "You're a doll! Super-duper chicken after all. The way you were talking I was afraid you were going to cop out. Now if you'll play the hostess, I'll put the casserole on warm and be back shortly."

Alone, Sherry felt diminished by the larger-than-life ancestral portraits staring down at her from the walls. The late-day sun shone through the windows that she had polished so painstakingly yesterday, highlighting the elaborate carving on the chairs and settees and corner hutch. It also showed up the frayed condition of the upholstery and silk lampshades, but when the sun set and the Club gathered, who'd notice?

Voices on the porch.

"How come you didn't come with Sherry? You always have before."

"I . . . I . . . had some work to do."

"Huh? Sherry said you were playing tennis. Is there something wrong? You used to go everywhere together."

"Excuse me," Kent said, and Sherry heard hurried footsteps in the hall.

Sherry felt the heat rise to her face. But she must not let her feelings get out of hand. With Jill in the dining room and Tina in the kitchen, this was her chance to talk to Kent alone.

"Hi!" She greeted him with a smile.

"Hello," he said uneasily.

"I'm glad you got here early."

Kent looked relieved, and she was glad she hadn't berated him for not picking her up.

"The chips and dip go there." She pointed to the marble-top table. The bowl of dip slid across the plate and he muttered.

"Oh, Kent, sit down and relax. We have lots of catching up to do."

He gravitated toward the settee and she wished he'd chosen something more comfortable, but she sat down next to him on the unyielding seat. His head ducked forward and his lids dropped over his eyes like a curtain, but not before she'd seen the anguish in them. She tried to put him at ease.

"I brought your favorite, the super-duper chicken." She smiled. "Tina told me that she saw you go back for three helpings last year."

"She said that? Next thing she'll be calling me Meatloaf Halliday."

"Oh, she didn't mean it that way. She just meant that you liked it better than the casseroles the other kids brought."

"I must have."

Sherry had hoped for a little more enthusiasm but maybe she'd gone at it wrong. Who likes to be reminded of what a pig he'd been — even if it had been a year ago?

The grandfather clock struck the hour. So much for small talk. Before the others came, she had to get the prom settled.

"Now about the prom." She looked at Kent closely but he seemed to withdraw, and she couldn't even be sure he was hearing the words that she had thought out so carefully. "Brian is crazy about the dress Tina ordered for the grand march, but I have a problem. Mom's trying to get me into a sweet-sixteen bridesmaid's dress that's the pits. Anyway, if you don't want your girl in a drippy dress, speak up and I'll find something we both like."

She paused and he said nothing, so she moved closer. "How about it?" she said.

"How about what?"

She had meant to keep calm, but her voice

rose, shards of anger piercing the air between them. "You mean you haven't been listening?"

"Sure. You were running on about Tina and her dress, and then about your dress that was drippy."

"Dresses for the prom." She emphasized the word prom. "Have you got the tickets yet?"

"No, not yet."

"It's less than a month away." Last year he'd made sure. *I don't want anyone snatching my girl.* Of course this year they had exchanged rings and maybe that made the prom automatic, but she decided to pin the matter down. "We'll go with Tina and Brian. And don't forget they lined us up for the class picnic, too."

"Yeah," Kent said. "Brian is after me to drive the wagon."

"I just love the dunes," Sherry said. "Didn't we have fun last year?"

"That was last year," Kent said, and Sherry felt chilled.

"We'll have just as much fun this year."

"I hope so," he said. Seeing the deep furrows scoring his forehead, Sherry hated Jill for what Jill was doing to him — and to her.

Voices in the hall.

"Gee, Midge, where'd you find that dumb outfit?" she heard Tina's sister say.

"If you don't like it, that's something in its favor," Midge replied.

Sherry jumped up. She wasn't up to talking to Midge. Let Kent cope.

"I'm going to help Tina," Sherry said, disappearing into the hall and heading for the kitchen. Tina was arranging radish roses, celery, and carrot curls on a crystal plate.

"Anything I can do?"

"Get the olives out of the fridge."

It was an old-fashioned kitchen with wooden counters, a wooden table, planked floors, and a lean-to ice house that had been converted into a pantry with floor-to-ceiling shelves.

The doorbell rang and rang again.

"That's the way it goes. Everyone arriving at once. Now if only Brian —"

"Did I hear my name?" Brian carried a case of soda through the back door. "I bought it cold. Saves messing around with ice."

"Every little bit helps." Tina turned to Sherry. "Now if you'll see what everyone wants. There's Coke and Fresca and orange, and if anyone's on a diet that's too bad."

Sherry moved among her friends, writing the orders on a scratch pad. Kent seemed more like himself now that he was in a corner talking drive shafts with Tubby. Midge cranked the handle of the Victrola and played old 78s.

"Listen, guys! Did you ever hear a voice like that? Caruso makes Pavarotti sound second rate."

"Pavarotti? What about gorgeous Placido Domingo?"

"Who needs opera? Give me rock and roll!"

The soda was gone. The relishes and the

dips gone. On cue, like a curtain rising, the door to the dining room opened.

"Wow!" Tina said.

Kent whistled.

Sherry's eyes traveled the length of the room and she felt disoriented — as if she'd made the wrong turn into the wrong house. Where were the long mahogany table, the dazzling chandelier with crystal pendants, the richly grained walnut wainscoting? She blinked. It was all there, only now the table was camouflaged under a red-and-white checked cloth, and the chandelier hidden behind a barrage of balloons. The dark walls were overlaid with bright posters lettered, BLOCK CLUB.

A raucous voice. "Chow down! Chow down!"

Sherry was certain she'd never heard the voice before. It had a hollow sound as if the words were bouncing around in an echo chamber. A ventriloquist?

"Hey!" Midge said. "Who's that?"

Jill giggled. "The new butler."

"Chow down. Step lively, mates. Chow down."

"Gotcha!" Tina cried and dashed to the corner serving table. She lifted the dropleaf and brought out a cage.

"Oh, Jill," she exploded, "what a panic! Where'd you ever dig up a talking parrot?"

"Gam knows all the right people. She borrowed Polly from the bouncer at the Hideaway, who got her from a retired seaman.

And believe me, when Polly doesn't like something her language can be salty."

"Wild!" Tubby poked his finger through the bars, but when the curved beak made a dive for it he withdrew it hastily.

Polly swore in English, Portuguese, and German.

"See what I mean?" Jill said. "Polly demands her pound of flesh."

"I don't have much to spare," Tubby said, "but I'd rather donate it to the Red Cross."

Kent leaned over the cage. "Polly want a finger?"

"Bug off," Polly said.

Kent laughed and Sherry laughed, too. Fun — a carnival with blocks and balloons and a parrot, every detail accounted for, even to Jill's red-checked skirt and T-shirt stenciled BLOCK CLUB, to match the decor. Everything perfect. *Too perfect*. An inner voice bombarded Sherry with questions. Why had Jill gone to so much trouble? If she were spending the rest of her life in Pineridge, she might go overboard to make her mark. But for someone on her way to Singapore, why the big splash?

Sherry had no answer.

"This way!" Tina presided over the buffet with its casseroles, salads, cakes, and pies. "Hurry, before it gets cold."

Tubby was first in line. Sherry fell in behind him and Kent followed her. Tubby loaded his plate with super-duper chicken but Kent took only a bite-sized portion, going right for the seafood casserole that Tina said Jill had brought.

"Didn't you say seafood didn't agree with you?" Sherry said.

"That was last year."

Sherry pictured Kent covered with red, itchy hives. But if that's the way he wanted it! She moved along the table, heaping greens on her plate.

"My favorite. Caesar salad!"

"What'll it be?" Tina wielded a knife above the chocolate angel food and the key lime pie.

"Later," Sherry said, and turned to Kent. "Where should we sit?"

"Anywhere you like," he said.

But when she reached the big table she saw the building blocks above each place spelling out each name. It couldn't be — but, yes, there was S-H-E-R-R-Y down at the foot of the table between Tubby and Chippie!

"There must be some mistake." She spoke loudly and distinctly. Everyone stopped and stared. "Kent and I always sit together."

Jill was first to recover. "Oh," she said, "I thought it would be more fun to mix things up a bit. Anyway, you and Kent will be seeing each other for the rest of your lives, so I didn't think you'd mind sharing him with me for one little dinner."

Sherry did mind, but she wasn't about to make a scene.

"I want to be fair about this," Jill said. "We'll flip. Who's got a dime?"

Sherry tried to catch Kent's attention, but

he was staring at the ceiling. Wasn't he aware of what was going on?

"Go on, Brian," Jill said. "Flip. Heads I'll change the table around. Tails it stays the same. Right, Sherry?"

"Tails! Tails! Tails!" Polly squawked, and everyone cracked up.

Sherry felt the floor tilt.

"Are you okay?" Kent was at her side, holding her elbow.

"Of course I'm okay." Sherry forced a smile.

"So I'm sitting at the head of the table for an hour. You don't care, do you?"

"Why would I?" she answered.

"Only because we like to sit together. Right?"

Sherry backed away. If he liked to sit with her so much, why hadn't he stepped up and changed the places around?

"It'll be fun sitting with Tubby for a change," she said.

"Gee, thanks." Tubby was on his feet looking pleased. "I know I'll like sitting next to you," he said as he pulled out her chair. She gestured toward the still-empty chair. "How come we're saddled with Chippie?"

"Remember — Midge has a hang-up about thirteen."

"I'm getting that way, too," she said.

THIRTEEN

"Sherry, is something wrong?"

Ms. Adams walked out from behind her desk and propped herself against the other side so she was face to face with Sherry.

Ms. Adams, her favorite teacher. If Sherry had a sister she'd like her to be just like Ms. Adams. She was fun and smart and pretty. But other teachers were fun and smart and pretty. Sherry looked into the warm gray eyes and tried to decide what made Ms. Adams so special. Maybe it was what was happening to her now. Ms. Adams hadn't flunked her, which she most certainly deserved. No, when she'd failed to hand in her paper on *The Great Gatsby* for the third time, Ms. Adams made no threats. She suggested that Sherry stay after school for a little chat.

"Not really wrong," Sherry answered her at last. "Not like I have mono or something."

"Tell me." Ms. Adams nodded encouragingly.

"Well, it's like this." Sherry fumbled with her eraser. "I turn on the reading lamp. I have my notebook and my ballpoint ready. I start to read. Sometimes I read one chapter and sometimes five, and after I finish I close the book — you won't believe me but I can't recall one word." Sherry pressed her temples. "All my life I've heard the saying, my mind is a blank. That's the way my mind is and there doesn't seemed to be a thing I can do about it."

"When did all this blankness start?"

"Maybe I've always had a tendency that way, only now it's getting worse."

Ms. Adams laughed, and the dimples in her cheeks deepened. "Not always," she said. "I gave you an A last semester and I give A's only to a privileged few. And you did win the school essay contest — with seniors competing — which proves that a panel of judges also consider your work superior."

Sherry propped her elbows on her desk and dropped her head in her hands. Her hair swung forward, and it occurred to her that she hadn't shampooed it in three days.

"I don't know what's the matter with me."

"I'm going to believe that you have tried to study and to do your term paper and to prepare for your tests. So rather than spoil your fine record with a failing grade, I will give you an incomplete."

"Thank you, Ms. Adams."

"On one condition. That you see your family physician."

"A doctor can't help me. No one can help me," she said quietly. Sherry got up and walked out of the room.

"Is something wrong, Sherry?"

Mr. Geezer came out from behind the counter and looked her in the eyes.

"I can't sleep," she said.

"I reckon you've been studying too hard. My grandson is always telling me what a star you are. What you should do is to take things a little easier."

"Mr. Geezer," she said impatiently, "what can you give me for insomnia?"

"I always say the best cure for insomnia is walking three miles. If you don't fall asleep right then, a tepid bath followed by a glass of warm milk —"

"Mr. Geezer, I need a sleeping pill. Something to knock me out cold."

Mr. Geezer backed off. "Sherry, don't expect me to hand you some drug under the counter. I knew your grandfather. A fine gentleman and my friend. He'd turn over in his grave."

"I didn't ask for anything illegal. I just want to go to sleep. Don't you understand that I can't sleep? I just keep wandering around all night and finals are coming up and all my papers are due and I just have to sleep."

Mr. Geezer patted her shoulder. "There, there, Sherry. I don't know what's keeping you awake, but before you start on pills, take my advice and see the doctor."

"I don't need a doctor. I just want to sleep!"

"Is something wrong, Sherry?"

"What do you mean, Mom?"

"Well, you're so silent every night at dinner and you hardly eat a thing; then you lock yourself in your room right after dinner and study. Now don't misunderstand me. We're very proud of you and your scholastic achievements, and we want you to do well on your exams, but there isn't a college in the world that's worth going to pieces over."

Sherry swallowed. "Is that what's happening to me?"

"We think you seemed much more relaxed when Kent was coming over to study with you. We can understand that Kent took a lot of your time, time that you need for your own papers and projects, but we wonder if you wouldn't be happier if you put your life back in balance. We want you to be happy, Sherry."

"Balance!" Sherry's voice cracked. "Life isn't a mathematical equation that adds up right!"

"Now, Sherry," Mom's cheeks paled, "I

think it's time we went to Dr. Sanders for a checkup."

"Dr. Sanders can't help me! I know it. Why doesn't everyone stop telling me to go to the doctor?"

FOURTEEN

"Sherry," Mom called, "the phone's for you."

Sherry yawned and swung her feet to the floor and reached for the phone on the desk.

"How are you doing?" Tina asked.

"Great."

"Did you see the doctor?"

"I had no choice. Dad said if I wouldn't go he'd ask Dr. Sanders to the house, and I couldn't hack that."

Tina cleared her throat. "What did Doc say?"

"No big deal. He said he wasn't a shrink and he wasn't interested in my hang-ups, but obviously I had a problem that I couldn't handle and was working myself into a state of stress — like half the kids in Pineridge."

"So what else is new. Around exam time, especially. The question is, what did he do for you?"

"He gave me some iron and some vitamins and some breathing exercises that work wonders. He told me not to press at home or school and to rest in the afternoons." Sherry plumped up the pillow in back of her head. "Now for the good news. He says the whole thing will pass —"

"When?" Tina asked eagerly.

" 'Give it a month,' he said, but I'm so much better already."

"Well enough to come to Block Club tonight?"

"Sure, I'll be there."

"Super. We really missed you last time."

"It's nice to be missed."

"Sherry?"

"Yeah?" Sherry knew what was coming, but she didn't know how to turn Tina off. She held the receiver away from her ear and concentrated on other sounds: Joey barking, the screech of a jay, the swishing of the wind in the big pines.

Tina talked rapidly. "You have no idea how worried I've been that it was something that happened at the potluck that set you off. I know you and Kent always sit together and Jill changed that, but after all she's new to Pineridge ways. I had a long talk with her afterward and she's really sorry. She says you're the best friend she's ever had. That it was you who brought her home when she had no place to go, and for all the world she wouldn't do anything to upset you."

Tina went on and on and the nice part was that the words blurred in Sherry's mind and she made no attempt to set the record straight. When at last Tina was through explaining what a good scout Jill was, Sherry put the phone back on the desk. She took a magic marker and crossed out one more day on the calendar with a big, black X.

Give it a month, Doc Sanders had said.

In less time than that Jill would be gone. All Sherry had to do was ride it out. She fingered the ring on its chain and felt comforting warmth in the touch of gold against her skin.

Mom was in the kitchen slicing green beans on the chopping board. Soon the garden beans would ripen on the vine and Sherry would pick them and they would be so deliciously tender Mom would cook them whole.

"When's dinner?" Sherry asked from the doorway.

Mom turned, fresh and pretty in pale lilac. "Any time after your father gets home. "Why?"

"It's Block Club night."

Mom put down the paring knife. "Are you sure you want to go, Sherry? If the doctor thinks you need extra rest, I wonder if it's a good idea to put yourself in a stressful situation."

"It's only the Block Club, Mom. Just my friends."

"But you were with your friends that night at Tina's." She added hastily, "I know you didn't want to talk about it at the time, but if you could ever bring yourself —"

"Please, not tonight, Mom."

"I only want to help, Sherry. It isn't like you to be unhappy. There has to be a reason."

Sherry's voice rose. "Lay off, Mom, will you?" She swallowed. "Sorry, Mom. You've got to understand. It's something I've got to work out for myself."

Mom went back to the cutting board. "All I know is that ever since that girl arrived from London you haven't been acting like yourself. And now Kent is behaving strangely. Just yesterday I was walking down the hill to town and he was walking up. And can you believe it? He brushed past me with a grunt. It isn't like Kent to be so rude."

"Look, Mom, I'd rather not discuss Kent." Sherry ran a cloth over the counter, which was already spotless. No, she didn't want to discuss Kent. She didn't want to even think about him. But he was in her thoughts all the same. Tina had phoned every day since she'd been sick. Midge and Brian and Tubby phoned. Even The Geek had called and said he'd missed her at school. But no word from Kent. Didn't he care for her at all? And if he didn't, why must she care so much for him? She wadded up the cloth in her fist and squeezed it until her knuckles whitened. Had Jill bewitched him?

Sherry looked out from under her lashes. "Say, Mom, do you believe in hypnotism?"

"If someone is willing to be hypnotized, I believe the power of suggestion can take effect."

"Suppose someone doesn't want to be hypnotized?"

"It's been proven that it is practically impossible to hypnotize an unwilling subject."

"What about exorcism? Do you believe someone can drive out evil spirits?"

"There are a few such cases on record."

"Well, if you can drive out evil spirits, is there a way you can invest someone with evil spirits? You know, the evil eye."

Mom laughed. "Really, Sherry, we all have demons enough without asking for more. What brought this on?"

"Oh, just something I read," Sherry said airily, and changed the subject. "What's for dinner?"

"I made a chicken casserole."

"I can't eat chicken."

"What do you mean you can't eat chicken? Chicken's always been your favorite."

"I know. But I can't eat it now. The very thought of chicken makes me sick. I'm sorry. There'll be that much more for you and Dad."

"But, Sherry" — Mom's eyes were concerned — "what do you feel like eating?"

"Something light. Cheerios, maybe."

"Cheerios for dinner?"

"If I'm hungry, I'll make a sandwich when I get back."

"Sherry," Mom said sternly, "how much weight have you lost? Five pounds? Ten?"

"Oh, not that much." Sherry smiled. "Take my word for it. In a couple of weeks everything will be just as it's always been."

Mom smiled back.

She brushed her hair until it shone. Spun gold, Kent had called it, and when he'd kissed her good night he caressed her hair with his fingertips. With a pang she set the brush down. She pulled on her jeans. Mom was right. She'd lost weight too fast. Her jeans were so loose she had to hike them up with a safety pin. She searched her closet for the embroidered peasant blouse to cover up the offending tuck. She glanced hesitantly in the dresser mirror. She looked paler than she liked, but once she'd applied a blusher to her cheeks and eyeshadow to her lids she was ready to face her friends.

Tonight wouldn't be easy, with Jill and Kent seated side by side in the back row where for so many years she and Kent had sat together. Would her friends pity her? She couldn't stand that. Would they talk behind her back? No doubt they were already doing it.

Her eyes lingered over the heap of pillows on her bed. If only she could curl up with a book of poetry and listen to her favorite tapes! But she wasn't going to let herself give in. She forced one foot ahead of the other, walking through the house and out into the garden.

"Here I come, Jill, ready or not."

What was there to worry about? It was only a game Jill and Kent were playing and the game was almost over. The heavy-headed peonies nodded encouragement. She opened the gate onto the road. The air was laced with mock orange, and the breeze was soft and languorous. The breathing exercises she'd done before setting out were having such a soothing effect that when Jill came jogging down the road and she saw Kent join her — falling right in step with her — Sherry merely felt her heart thud.

I'll hang back a minute, she decided. She waited for Mrs. Brophy and Joey to navigate the road, Mrs. Brophy moving cautiously over the ruts and Joey bouncing around her like a rubber ball.

"What's with you, Joey?" Sherry leaned over and patted his head. "You've shrunk since the last time I saw you."

Mrs. Brophy smiled. "Joey had his first haircut, and the girl in Poodle Paradise said she'd rather trim a tiger. But now I can see a resemblance to his father, who's a champion — not that I ever want to show Joey."

Sherry tried to keep her mind on Joey, but like a magnet to a steel pin, her eyes were drawn to Kent and Jill. She watched as they sprinted along the path through the meadow, Jill running easily, Kent pressing to keep up.

"I'd better go," Sherry said, "before they lock me out."

"Dear, dear. I hope there's no penalty for tardiness."

"Oh, no. The Block Club's just for fun."

At that moment Joey gave an excited bark and tugged on the leash. Mrs. Brophy lurched forward and Joey jerked free, racing toward the woods in pursuit of a rabbit.

"Come back, Joey! Come back!" Mrs. Brophy cried, but Joey only raced faster.

Sherry's heart stood still. Even if Kent said all rabbits were a nuisance and should be shot, she loved the little furry creatures. She felt a sense of thanksgiving when the rabbit stretched his body, flattened his ears, and made a flying leap into the underbrush, escaping the little poodle.

"I didn't know I'd bought a hunting dog." Mrs. Brophy looked distressed.

"Any dog'll chase a moving object. Anyhow, the rabbit got away."

Mrs. Brophy eyed the woods. "I'll never get Joey back now."

"Of course you will. I can catch him easily with that leash trailing behind."

Sherry found him sniffing around a juniper bush. "Don't you know Br'er Rabbit got away?" she teased. She gathered Joey in her arms and returned him to Mrs. Brophy.

"It's obedience training for you, Joey," Mrs. Brophy scolded, but when he licked her chin her voice melted. "Oh, I'm glad to have you back." Her eyes went to Sherry. "And a special thank you, my dear. How much better the world would be if everyone were as helpful as you!"

With Mrs. Brophy's words ringing in her ears, Sherry set off across the meadow, her step livelier than usual, her heart pumping faster. Wading through the knee-high grass amid clumps of chicory and wild asters that accented the field in pockets of purples and pinks, her mind spun back to the summer she and Kent were six. *Our flower summer.* They'd turned their Secret Place into a bower, and she'd made flower wreaths and necklaces and bracelets and fancied herself a wood nymph.

"Better than jewels." She had held out her arm entwined in vines and blossoms for Kent to admire.

"Except for the ants," Kent said.

Her mind drifted pleasantly. She and Kent shared a lifetime of memories. Their relationship ran deep like a river. Jill was a sputtering motorboat making noise, making waves, creating a disturbance. In a little while the churning would be over and the river would ebb and flow, smooth as before.

For a long moment, Sherry stared at the closed clubhouse door psyching herself up. With head high, she eased inside.

"Welcome!" Tina stopped in midsentence.

Everyone clapped enthusiastically and although Sherry didn't look back, she was almost sure the loudest clapping of all was coming from the back row where Kent was sitting.

"Sorry I'm late." Sherry sat down, more than a little relieved that her friends seemed genuinely happy that she'd returned. "Joey chased a rabbit into the woods and I retrieved him for Mrs. Brophy, and it took a while."

"You haven't missed much, and it's nice to know that one of us has done a good deed for a change." Tina looked around. "Any new business?"

Midge launched into a progress report on the sell-yourself auction. Sherry only half-listened. The auction seemed a millennium away. She had more immediate problems to face up to. If she and Kent had drifted apart, was she partly to blame? Was it enough to stand on the sidelines waiting for Jill to leave? Was anything to be gained by crawling into a shell? She'd always been friendly and outgoing, completely at ease with Kent. After seventeen years, didn't she know him well enough to ask him to explain himself?

Of course it would be nice if he had volunteered to talk over his feelings with her, but that was the last thing Kent would ever do. She had hoped to reach him at the potluck, but Chippie's nasty remarks had put him in a defensive mood and what little conversation they'd had bombed. Besides, parties were no place for a heart-to-heart.

Midge waved for attention. "At the last meeting we agreed the auction should be held July fifteenth. Now Dad's talking about a vacation that week so if you want me to run things, we have to move the auction back or ahead. All in favor of the earlier date —"

Sherry raised her hand. Once the auction was over, the rest of the summer would be free. She closed her eyes and dreamed of last year when she and Kent and Tina and Brian had cruised around the countryside. This summer would be the same, wouldn't it?

"The earlier date has it," Midge said.

"Is there any further business?" Tina rapped the gavel. "If not, will someone please move the meeting be adjourned?"

"I so move." A bass voice from the back row. She'd know that voice anywhere. She didn't turn, but waited until Jill and Kent were outside. It was the hour between daylight and dark, when the purple sky was deepening into the shades of night with a pale moon floating above, but no stars visible.

"C'mon," Jill said to Kent, "let's go."

"Wait," Sherry stepped out of the shadows.

Kent swung slowly around to face her. What was he thinking? What was he feeling? He managed a half-smile.

"Hi!"

"Where've you been keeping yourself?" Jill said cheerfully. Sherry wondered how she could have let this girl with the shaggy hair and baggy running pants intimidate her.

"I wasn't feeling well. Now I'm fine."

"If you want to keep on feeling good, take up jogging. You'd be surprised —"

"Jogging is something I can do without."

"Try karate then."

"I'm not interested in black belts."

"But it can be useful." Jill carried on despite the fact that neither she nor Kent encouraged her. "Gam relies on bouncers, but Mum insisted that I learn to defend myself. Good thing, too. I ran into this wolf in the park who thought I was easy pickings. I gave him the old karate treatment and that took care of him." Jill extended her leg. "The important thing is to keep the sole of the foot parallel to the ground and kick with the outside edge of the foot, like so —"

Sherry drew back, even though the side swipe was not meant for her. Was she always going to retreat when Jill was around?

"I think it's safe enough in Pineridge that I can do without defense training." Sherry spoke with spirit. She studied Kent, but suddenly it was dark and she couldn't read his expression. "Remember, Kent? You were trying to talk me into keeping a guard dog at our little cabin in the woods, and I told you I felt so safe in our woods that I didn't need a dog for protection. Right?"

"Right." Kent's voice was barely audible.

"Maybe you and I should get together," Sherry said.

"Why, sure."

Sherry had hoped he would say when, but at least he hadn't said that he wouldn't meet with her.

"How about Sunday night? Dad said he'd grill hamburgers on the patio, if the weather's okay."

Kent scuffed the path with the toe of his running shoe. "I'll let you know just as soon as I can," he said.

"By noon tomorrow," Sherry said, and was glad to hear such firmness in her voice.

FIFTEEN

Kent phoned before noon Saturday, and on Sunday he arrived at her house on time. He was so pleasant throughout supper that it was easy to forget that he had been neglecting her for Jill. But now that he'd come, she wasn't going to let him rush off without talking to him alone.

"Are you sure, Mom, you don't need help with the dishes?" Sherry popped the last bite of the walnut brownie in her mouth.

"We ate on paper plates so there wouldn't be a lot of dishes," Mom said.

"Then it's okay if Kent and I go for a walk in the woods?"

"It's lovely in the woods this time of year," Mom nodded.

Kent stiffened. Even though he was on the other side of the patio she could feel his resistance, but slowly his shoulders relaxed and she knew that he had decided to go along with her.

"Here, Sherry, take this." Dad reached for the bug repellent under his chair. "The mosquitoes were lethal down by the creek."

"Mosquitoes don't usually bother me," Sherry said, "but there's always a first time."

Kent stood up and flashed, first Mom and then Dad, one of his wonderful warm smiles. "Thanks for including me. Everything tastes so great cooked outside."

Once out the back gate, they headed like homing pigeons for their Secret Place. It was just as it had always been, two minds in the same groove. She didn't have to say, where shall we go, and he didn't have to say, what shall we do — they just knew.

It was darker in the woods with the sun threading through the leafy branches of oak and maple, through the needles of pine and hemlock, making dancing shadows on the path. The path was dry, but water stagnated in the hollow below. Across the water trillium and marsh violets poked up through the soggy, brown leaves like a wonderful surprise, and under a jack pine she spotted some early mushrooms.

"Look, Kent, what a find! Slippery jacks."

He touched her arm. "Not now, Sherry. It's too wet. We'll come back some other day with boots on."

Sherry noted the "we" and smiled.

When they reached the big oak, the path they were following veered off to Pine Creek, but the path to their Secret Place had completely disappeared.

"If you don't take care of something," Sherry said, "isn't it scary how fast nature takes over?"

Kent frowned. "I was sure I could walk right to it."

"It has to be around here someplace." Suddenly she stumbled.

"That's one way to find it. Now I can see what's happened. The bed of ferns spread right over the circle and the new crop of vines are climbing all over the stones."

"If I'd known, I'd have brought my machete," Kent said.

"We've always had the place in shape long before now." Not wanting to sound critical, she added, "Of course, there's still plenty of time."

"Yeah, all summer."

Sherry gestured. "Help yourself."

"Don't mind if I do." Kent lowered himself onto the biggest, flattest rock and stretched out his legs. Perching on the smaller stone next to him, she experienced a sudden rush of emotion.

"Remember, Kent, how we always came here when something went wrong in our lives? School . . . family . . . friends. The peace had a healing effect. I'll never forget the day your father remarried — well, you just wouldn't leave."

Kent dropped his head in his hands. "It

was so soon. I don't know how he could have done it."

"Now, Kent, you know your father's been wonderful to you — taking you in the family business, letting you borrow the wagon any time you want it. And no curfew. At my house, there's rules, rules, rules. Mom has a way of treating me like I'm seven, instead of seventeen and practically engaged."

She hoped the word engaged would trigger some kind of response. But Kent busied himself squashing a spider.

"Maybe we'd better come back some other time after I've cleared the jungle away."

"No, Kent. You're going to stay right here and talk to me. You haven't phoned me. You haven't been over to study with me. You haven't sat with me in the cafeteria. And you don't want to sit with me at the Block Club." She made eye-to-eye contact. "What gives?"

Kent rubbed the palms of his hands together in a gesture of despair.

"It's Jill," he said.

"Everyone knows that."

"Try to understand, Sherry —"

"Why should I?"

"My feelings for her have nothing to do with my feelings for you. She's got me all mixed up. Most of the time I don't know whether I'm coming or going. I've never known anyone like her before, and I can't seem to see enough of her. She's unique. One of a kind. Fearless. Not afraid to stand up to Miss Hatcher or expose a phony like Madame

Joneau. Not afraid to attack a man twice her size. But, Sherry, you know it's always been you."

"I can't see you with Jill," Sherry said calmly. "For years you've been telling me that you can't stand people who make scenes, and Jill's always in the middle of one. A show-off of the worst kind."

"Don't you see? Jill's different from everyone else. She has my sympathy. It's been a rough go for her all the way. I lost one parent and that's been hard on me. But Jill not only lost her real father but has had to put up with two stepfathers, and Sir is a tyrant." Kent shifted on the stone. "You can't judge until you've been there. What would you know? You've got it made. A super father, a loving mother, all of you together forever and so close."

Sherry felt her cheeks heat up. "What are you trying to tell me, Kent? That you love Jill and you no longer love me?"

Kent reared back. "I never said any such thing! I just said Jill needs me and I want to help her through these last days, and I don't see why you have to make such a big thing of it."

"So you're telling me to be a good guy and just hang around until Jill departs. I'm not at all sure I'm going to buy that."

"Nothing of the sort." Kent stood up and pulled her to her feet and pressed his lips against hers. She knew she loved him too much to give him up.

SIXTEEN

All the while Sherry was making sandwiches for the class picnic she dreamed of
the Secret Place, with the branches curving
above her and the stones circling around her
marking the spot where the foundation of
their cabin would be. She dreamed of Kent's
arms around her and his kiss and his promise
that everything was as it had always been between them. He had even started phoning
her again, and she had been lulled into believing everything was right between them.
Now for the past week, silence.

There was a time I could count on you,
Kent. She slid sandwiches for two into plastic
bags. *But how can I now?*

"Of course you can count on Kent," Tina
had assured her yesterday. "He'll pick me up
first and then meet you on Back Road by the
linden at ten o'clock sharp."

"How can I believe that? I understand he's

been seeing Jill every afternoon and evening all week."

"If you ask me, it's big of him to show her around these last few days when we all know he'd much rather be with you."

Sherry took a deep breath. "Yeah, really big."

"Quit stewing," Tinā said. "Sir is in the midst of negotiating for a luxury apartment on the outskirts of Singapore and just as soon as school is out Jill will jet to the Malay peninsula."

Jet right out of my life. Sherry's heart soared off into space like the needle-nosed Concorde.

The phone rang. Sherry braced herself. No doubt Kent was coming up with some last-minute excuse to dump her. But the caller was Mrs. Brophy.

"My dear, in appreciation of your taking care of Joey when I had that virus, I have a little present for you."

"Oh, Mrs. Brophy, that's so sweet of you. I'd love to come over now, but I'm just on my way to Sleeping Bear Dunes."

"I can hardly remember when I was young enough to climb that mountain, but do have fun. Joey and I will look for you sometime soon."

Maybe sooner than you think, Sherry admitted to herself. She carted the cooler to the appointed place, waiting for Kent. She was so sure he wouldn't come, it was almost a shock when the wagon rolled around exactly at ten with Tina and Brian already in the backseat.

For a brief second she let herself believe that it was just like it had always been, the four of them going off for the day together. Last summer had been special — in celebration of getting their drivers' licenses they'd spread their wings trying new places and new things, paddling down the Au Sable, waterskiing on Walloon, fishing on Lake Charlevoix.

Now easing into the front seat beside Kent, she wondered what this summer would bring. When Jill goes, will it be the same?

"We're in luck," Sherry said, "not a cloud in the sky."

"Yep," Brian agreed. "That big pile of sand can sure raise Cain. Fluky winds and whopping storms."

Kent said nothing, not even hello. He concentrated on the road as if he were fighting rush hour traffic, when in reality the few cars they passed lumbered along under luggage racks, trailing cycles and boats.

Anger like hot steam boiled up inside her. Who was this sullen stranger at her side?

"Kent," she said quietly, "I've been looking forward to this day, and if you're going to clam up and sulk you can just turn around and take me home. I'll ride with someone else, or I just may stay and go over to Mrs. Brophy's. She has a surprise for me."

"No, no," he said hastily. "It's just that —"

"Just what?"

"Something that's been eating me. Something that's been keeping me awake nights."

"Don't tell me about wakeful nights," she said.

He lifted his eyes briefly from the road and blurted out, "There's a rumor going around that you were the one who put that item in the "Guess Who?" column in the school weekly."

"I don't know what you're talking about."

"I do," Tina said merrily. "I thought it was funny."

"I haven't seen the paper in ages."

"It was a week ago," Brian said, and Sherry knew that he'd noticed the item, too.

"The accused has a right to know what she is being accused of," Sherry said. "Tell me."

"It was a cheap shot," Kent said.

"Well, if that's all Kent has to say, I'll give it to you," Tina announced. "It went something like this: *'Who's the member of the tennis team who plays doubles on the court and plays double-cross afterward? Does he think his London lass has pull at Wimbledon?'*"

Sherry jerked forward against her shoulder belt and glared at Kent. She didn't know whether she was more angry or more hurt. "So you jumped to the conclusion that I was the one who planted the story?"

Kent's neck reddened. "I was told you had."

"By Jill, I suppose."

"She just repeated what she'd heard."

"Kent, why would you listen to her? Why didn't you phone me and ask me right out?"

"I should have, Sherry, I know. I just don't know what's the matter with me these days." He reached over. "Forgive me?"

The car swerved.

"Hey!" Tina said. "No one-arm driving. Kiss and make up on your own time."

"I'd like that," Kent said.

Sherry laughed. Tina said Sherry's laugh was contagious and started laughing, too, then Kent laughed and the tension that had sparked between them evaporated. The air cleared. Communication was restored. Now Sherry knew what she had only suspected, — that Kent's strange, mercurial moods and their misunderstandings were touched off by Jill, who was forever feeding Kent half-truths and out-and-out lies.

Sherry leaned back and closed her eyes, her head rocking with the motion of the car. Feeling tuned in to Kent, she sent him a message. *If you want the truth, come to me as you always have.*

She must have dozed, for Brian's voice rang in her ears like an alarm. She emerged through layers of sleep and looked out the window at the woods flashing by.

"Turn north at Empire," Brian directed.

"Already? Only a few more miles?" Sherry said surprised. Kent was a super driver. She never felt secure enough with Brian or Tina driving to fall asleep.

Tina said, "I'm going to tell you all the story of *The Three Bears*, but not the oldie about Mama and Papa and Baby Bear."

"Must you?" Brian made a face.

Sherry smiled. Nothing had changed. Tina telling one of her funky stories and Brian objecting.

"This one goes with the picnic," Tina said, gesturing toward Lake Michigan. "Once upon a time there was a forest fire on the other side of the lake, so Mother Bear and her two cubs started the long swim across to safety on the other shore. Mother Bear reached land safely and lay down on the sand to sleep while waiting for her cubs to arrive. But a few miles offshore the cubs were too tired to swim farther and they drowned."

"A cheerful little yarn," Brian said.

"Shh. I'm not finished. Manitou, the Great Spirit, took pity on the mother and marked the spot of their sinking with an island for each cub, North Manitou and South Manitou."

"And how did Mother Bear take to the real estate deal?"

"Mother Bear still sleeps and waits. Get it? — Sleeping Bear Dunes."

"I'd rather not," Kent said. "I never did think the green stuff growing on top of the dune looked much like a bear anyway." He stopped the car at the visitors' station and found out that the dune buggies were not operating.

"At least we had a ride last summer."

Sherry remembered the jeeplike wagon, with huge balloon tires that drove around the top of the dunes, stopping at the scenic overlooks.

"I'd rather climb anyway," Tina said. "That's what the other kids are doing."

"I don't mind going up," Sherry said. "It's coming down —"

"Don't worry," Kent said. "We'll slide down, a little at a time. I'll be with you every inch of the way."

That was what was so great about Kent. She didn't have to explain that she was squeamish about heights. He always understood.

They parked the car and she and Tina transferred the lunch from the cooler to the backpacks the boys had strapped on.

"We could eat lunch at the picnic table." Sherry looked with longing at the tables spread out under the trees at the foot of the dunes.

"What! We can do that any old time. It's over the top for us," Kent said.

Sherry contemplated the massive sand heap. It looked twice as big as she remembered it.

"How high is it anyway?"

Kent shrugged, but Brian's computer brain spewed out, "Four hundred and eighty feet, high as a forty story building, the largest living sand dunes in the world."

"What I'd like to know," Tina said, "is when is a sand dune living and when is a sand dune dead?"

"Living sand dunes move. Sleeping Bear has already buried an abandoned town, covered up a forest and then uncovered it, and is still moving."

"I hope it won't make up its mind to mow down Pineridge," Tina said.

"We won't be around to find out," Brian said.

Kent kicked off his sneakers and made a running start for the sloping side of the dunes just as if he were about to plunge into a lake.

"Here goes!"

"Easy, man," Brian called after him. "Just because you're in good shape."

"We'll climb at our own pace." Sherry curled her toes into the warm, slippery sand. "He can wait for us at the top."

But after his initial sprint, Kent slowed down and they climbed four abreast. The climb was a series of stops and starts, ten steps up, two steps sliding backward.

"Coronary Hill." Sherry placed her hand over her pulsating heart.

"It's a tester," Kent said, "and you're doing great."

Sherry knew right then that she'd make it to the top.

"I'm glad we got a head start," Tina said breathlessly when they paused at the halfway mark. "See — the kids are just getting off the bus now. They look like ants way down there."

Sherry decided not to look.

The sun was overhead now, heating up the

mountain of sand, heating up their bodies. Sherry's T-shirt stuck to her ribs, but she was too tired to care.

They climbed more slowly and talked less.

Suddenly a lithe creature clambered up the sand on all fours — feet dug in, hands scrabbling the mountain side — and passed them by. *Jill!* She was scaling the dunes with the same ease as a monkey shins up a pole. She stood up only long enough to shout, "Better speed up, you guys, before your sandwiches fry."

"If you ask me," Tina said, "she has an ape for an ancestor."

"Maybe that, too," Sherry said. "Her grandfather was a stunt cyclist and did all kinds of nutty things."

"How would you know that?" Kent asked.

"Gam told me. She had to leave the jerk before he jumped over a canyon with Jill's mother, who was just a baby, strapped to his back."

"Jill never mentioned her grandfather to me," Kent said. There was hurt in his voice and it pained Sherry to hear it.

They made the final, exhausting push, and threw themselves down in the shade of a cottonwood, panting, sweating. Sherry flipped over and looked through the quivering leaves to the azure sky. Sand shimmered for miles, and beyond the sand were the never-ending blue green waters of Lake Michigan with a sailboat, spinnaker puffed out, skimming along the horizon. Idly she wondered where

Jill was. For sure, she hadn't collapsed under the first tree.

Kent recovered from the climb in no time. He stood up and waved for attention speaking in a stentorian voice. "Like Sir Edmund Hillary who planted a flag when he reached the pinnacle of Mt. Everest —"

"Hold it," Brian said. "This may be the world's largest living dune but the world's highest peak it ain't."

"Nevertheless," Kent intoned, "in commemoration of our successful feat, I hereby plant the Star and Stripes in this glade of trees." He removed a tiny flag from his backpack.

"How about that?" Sherry saluted and launched into "America the Beautiful," ending with "from sea to shining sea." She'd meant to ham it up, but the white-capped waters of Lake Michigan to the west and the smooth, sapphire waters of Glen Lake to the east really *were* so beautiful that she was overcome with wonder.

Tina leaned over and shook the sand out of her hair, and Sherry thought how gorgeous she was, deeply tanned even though summer hadn't officially started — a girl for all seasons.

"How would you like to hear the story about the penguin who was asked to dine at the White House?" Tina looked around hopefully.

"Positively no more stories until after lunch," Brian said.

They sat in the grove of trees eating warm sandwiches and drinking warm soda and loving it. Sherry looked around the little circle and experienced a sense of déjà-vu, and she knew it was because they'd sat together under other trees and shared other lunches. There was a bond between them that only strengthened with time.

"What are you thinking?" Kent reached for her hand. How long had it been since he'd reached for her hand? She was familiar with every lump and bump, but now she felt a new callous — tennis, perhaps.

"I'm thinking it's a perfect day," she said.

He gave her hand a gentle squeeze and she squeezed his back, and she knew by the tenderness of his touch that she was the one he loved.

Suddenly shrieks. Midge running pell-mell across the dunes toward them.

"You've got to come, Kent," Midge cried. "They're all betting she won't dare do it, but you know she will."

Kent frowned. "Do what?"

"Swing out over the bluff. Tubby volunteered to swing her and you know he'll drop her."

Sherry's stomach turned over. Even looking down the sheer drop-off to the shore of Lake Michigan had made her so dizzy last year she'd had to back off and lie down in the dune buggy. Now Jill was asking to be swung out over with just the grip of a couple of high school boys between her and a mile-long drop.

"Why me?" Kent said.

"You're the only one who could stop her, and if she won't be stopped at least you won't drop her."

"Oh, Kent! It's suicidal! Don't go!" Sherry pleaded.

He didn't seem to hear her. He was on his feet. A knight in shining armor off to rescue a damsel in distress.

"C'mon," Brian said to Tina. "Up and at 'em, where the action is."

"Why not?" Tina said, "but personally I don't think even Jill is that nutty."

Brian extended his hand to Sherry. "Coming?"

Sherry wanted no part of it. But she knew she couldn't just sit by herself under a cotton-wood tree while Kent was hanging over a cliff.

The sun was hot on her head and the sand burned her feet as she ran, but the core of her being was ice. Nightmares reeled before her eyes. Kent cartwheeling over the brink. Kent spinning through the air. Kent smashing on the boulders below.

All because of Jill.

The breeze freshened against her face and a flock of gulls wheeled overhead, and she knew they were nearing Lake Michigan. With a feeling of apprehension, she saw the crowd. Where had everyone come from? They were strangely silent and fear gnawed at her heart.

"I think I'm going to be sick," she told Brian.

Brian took her by the arm and the three of them moved forward together. Suddenly Brian stopped, his muscles tensed, and Sherry knew this was it. He muttered an expletive. "At least it isn't Kent holding her."

Sherry forced herself to look. A hefty jock held Jill by the hands. Another muscleman grasped Jill by the feet. Not Kent. Not Tubby — Sherry was grateful for that. Together they swung Jill out over the drop-off and back over the sand and out over the drop-off — Sherry's stomach flipped with each swing. *Out* . . . back . . . *Out* . . . back . . . *Out* . . .

"Okay, you guys!" Kent emerged from the crowd. "Put her down!"

One last swing and Jill was released on the sand. Everyone clapped and screamed and cheered. Jill bowed, raising her hands above her head, acknowledging the applause.

"Fun!" she cried. "Exhilarating! Thrills and chills! Who else would like to try?" Her eyes scanned the crowd and settled on Sherry. "What about you, Super Sherry? You don't have to swing forever. Only as long as you like."

Sherry felt the bile rise in her throat and quickly turned away.

SEVENTEEN

"Sherry," Tina boomed over the phone, "why didn't you tell me?"

"Tell you what?"

"About the prom dress. It just happened I was in Glory-Bee's picking up my dress when your mother came in and announced that she wanted the gown that had been in the window last week, and she didn't even ask the price."

"It wasn't my idea."

"Hey, I don't get it. For months you've been screaming that you wouldn't be caught dead in that bridesmaid's dress, and now your mother buys the dress of your dreams and you act as if you don't care."

"I told her not to."

"Are you crazy?"

"Why should I get all dressed up for someone who doesn't even phone me?"

"For heaven's sake, Sherry, I thought when

you exchanged rings that made things definite."

"So did I."

"Now, Sherry" — Tina took on her big sister voice, which always amused Sherry since Sherry was older by four months — "stop acting like a nit. Who cares if Kent phones every hour on the hour?"

"How does this grab you?" Sherry said. "Only one phone call since we went to the dunes."

"Oh."

In the long pause that followed, Sherry watched an ant climb up the drapes, straight up like scaling the dunes — only the ant seemed tireless.

"I don't understand," Tina said. "We all had such a good time together."

"Yes, a super day until —" Sherry broke off. "Why would anyone want to do such a crazy thing?"

"I understand she's done it before. On the Isle of Wight. That cliff was so high the only way to reach the beach was by chairlift. On a dare she let herself be hung over the edge, and the holiday crowd went wild."

"She does like the big scene," Sherry said.

"Look here, Sherry," Tina remonstrated, "all this has nothing to do with the prom. I happen to know that Kent is definitely planning on taking you and even if you're mad — and who can blame you — please be a good sport and go. Honest, it won't be any fun without you."

144

"I'll think about it."

"Sherry, you know Kent will be heart-broken if you back out."

"So —"

"Sherry, as a best friend I think I should set you straight. It's no secret that Jill and Kent are spending time together, but it's such a temporary thing, a little diversion, and it means nothing. It's you and only you he really cares about."

Sherry fingered the ring and glanced at the calendar with the dates crossed off. Jill would be gone — maybe in two days, in any case in less than two weeks. All she had to do was dress up, smile, and pretend everything was the same. But could she?

"I won't be going," she said, after a pause.

EIGHTEEN

Sherry leaned toward the mirror, pinning the corsage Kent had sent her on her shoulder strap. The sensuous fragrance of the gardenias put her in a romantic mood, reminding her of other proms, other nights.

Tonight her eyes were more violet than blue, and her sweep of hair, brightened by the summer sun, shone with iridescent lights. The pink and lavender cummerbund nipped in her full-skirted gown and pinpointed her tiny waist, now so small Kent could span it with his big hands.

She hadn't intended to go to the prom. She'd told Tina to forget it, and she'd told Mom to return the dress. But Mom refused and Tina kept on insisting and Kent wouldn't take no for an answer.

"Sherry, you promised me. We talked it

146

over at the potluck and you said it was definite, that arrangements had already been made for us to go to both the picnic and the prom with Tina and Brian."

"You hadn't even bought the tickets."

"I bought them the very next morning."

"Why didn't you tell me?"

"I did. Don't you remember?"

She didn't remember. But maybe he had told her. She hadn't been too swift at the time.

"Let's just say I've changed my mind."

"Please, Sherry. I really want to take you, and if you won't go that means I won't go, and Tina and Brian will be out in the cold, too."

"Well, if you're just dying to take me, how come I don't hear from you once in awhile?"

"I'm a louse. I don't handle things right. First the tennis coach tells me I'm not practicing enough. Then the tutor Dad hired tells me I'm not studying enough. Then Gam gets the flu and dumps the care and feeding of the cats on Jill, and she asks me to give her a hand."

"I see. You're all tied up with the cats."

"Just for now. Jill said she would have asked you, but you're allergic to cats."

"She said that?"

"Well, if I'm not phoning you all the time, it isn't that I'm not thinking of you." Kent's voice deepened with conviction. "Things will be different as soon as school is out."

"So I'm on the back burner for the time being."

"Never!" Kent sounded shocked.

Now as Sherry touched up her lips with silver pink gloss, she was glad that she'd let Kent persuade her to go. What could be more gruesome than sitting home on prom night with Dad and Mom feeling sorry for her?

The gym looked like a gym despite the efforts of the decorating committee. They had lavishly draped windows, walls, and basketball nets with green and white crepe paper, and festooned the bandstand with green and white — the school colors.

Sherry glanced around but there was no escaping the chaperones who held court inside the large double doors. She gave Tina a little shove.

"Go ahead. You're leading the grand march. That means you should be first." Sherry waited with Kent and when Tina and Brian were halfway down the line, they followed at a discreet pace.

"How pretty you look, Sherry." Mr. Rogers, head of the school board and a friend of her father's, nodded approval.

"A most becoming gown!" Midge's mother, chairman of the PTA, complimented Sherry, and compliments from her were hard to come by.

"How do you do?" Sherry smiled. She had forgotten the head librarian's name.

Last in line, Miss Hatcher, dressed in black with gunmetal stockings and sensible shoes, looking like an old crow among a covey of tropical birds.

Sherry extended her hand.

"Hur-rumph." Miss Hatcher grunted as she eyed Sherry and Kent coldly, and Sherry hurried on.

Once out of earshot, she said to Kent, "She is impossible."

"Agreed." When the music started up he looked at Sherry in that special way with one eyebrow up and one level. "Dance?"

Sherry slid into his arms. His hand pressed the small of her back and they moved together as one, gliding, dipping, whirling. Couples all around them — but it was just as if they were dancing alone, dancing together on their own enchanted isle.

The music stopped, and Sherry felt momentarily disoriented as a voice twanging over the loud speaker broke into her beautiful, private world.

"Now for the grand march! The grand march, that wonderful, long-standing Pineridge High tradition, by popular acclaim will be led this year by none other that Tina Trowbridge and her escort Brian Farley."

"Doesn't she look terrific?" Sherry said as Tina, in her flaming dress with a wreath of flowers crowning her shining black hair, promenaded the length of the gym arm in arm with Brian.

"She's not the only one." Kent's fingers slid up Sherry's bare arm.

Tina and Brian circled back and Sherry and Kent joined them on the right hand and Midge and Tubby on the left. On the next turnaround there were twelve abreast, and then twelve more couples fell in behind until everyone was in formation spread out across the wide, shining floor. As the music came to a crescendo they closed ranks, stomping and clapping.

Sherry pushed through the crowd around Tina.

"You were great!"

"Now, Sherry, anyone can walk down the gym and back."

"Not the way you walk." Sherry envied Tina her regal bearing.

The band launched into something swingy and this time they exchanged partners, Tina dancing with Kent and Sherry with Brian. Brian did his seesaw step, shifting his weight from left foot to right and back again. Sherry, who loved sweeping the whole dance floor, wondered how Tina put up with poor Brian's lack of coordination year after year and wished she were back in Kent's arms.

"You really had us worried," Brian swayed left, swayed right. "We took it for granted that you and Kent would be coming together like always so when you started backing off —"

"You know me better than that." Sherry

teetered from side to side, deciding that if you weren't really dancing you might as well talk. "I only backed off because we all know that Kent hasn't been around that much."

"Kent is nuts. He's got a gorgeous gal." Brian stopped moving altogether and held her at arm's length and looked at her appreciatively. "Just yesterday I gave him a piece of my mind."

"You did?"

"You bet. 'Kent,' I said, 'Play around with dynamite and you deserve to get blown up.'"

Sherry laughed. "And what did he say to that?"

"'Not to worry.'"

Left foot, right foot. "Oh, Brian, it won't ever come to that."

The music grew louder. A final fanfare and the band filed out for a break.

"Wow!" Tina said as she joined them. "Dancing with Kent is a matter of life and breath."

"How can you say that?" Kent made a face. "I wasn't even in high gear."

Sherry smiled. Each to his own. The faster Kent danced, the more exciting it was to her.

Kent gestured toward the refreshment stand. "Something cool?"

"Count us out." Tina looked into her compact mirror and rearranged the wreath that had gone askew. "Leading the grand march isn't all fun and games. We have to join the chaperones during each break."

"What about you, Sherry?"

"I could use a float."

"Try and find us a chair, will you?" Kent said.

He returned with the Coke floats just as she was sitting down. He pulled his chair closer and their eyes met above the tall paper cups.

"How now, Princess?"

Princess. Once upon a time he'd called her Princess and she'd believed him. Once upon a time he'd made her feel like one. Tonight he was trying to bring the magic back. Never, not for a single instant, had he taken his eyes off her while he danced with Tina.

"Kent," she began, but broke off when his attention suddenly veered. Even before she saw her, Sherry knew it had to be Jill. Questions raced through her mind. Why hadn't Jill come to the prom until now? Why was she rushing across the floor, the gold hem of her sari hiked up to her knees? And why was The Geek trailing reluctantly behind?

"Guess what?" Jill skidded to a stop. "I'm leaving."

"Oh, no!" Kent said.

"Oh, yes!"

"When?"

"The day after tomorrow."

Sherry's heart beat out the refrain, *It's over, over, over*.

"Kent, I've got to see you alone," Jill said.

Kent frowned. "Please, Jill —"

"It'll only take a sec. I know you'd rather be with Sherry, but in view of my imminent departure, I really must see you now."

The furrows deepened. "Can't it wait?"

"Why do you think I came to the prom when it's half over? Not to be with The Geek. I came because there's a question that only you can answer."

"Shoot."

"Not here, Kent. In private. This way."

Kent rose grudgingly, and Sherry looked at Jill with contempt. Even when Kent turned her off, she kept right at him.

"Save my seat, Sherry. I'll be right back."

But no sooner had he left than The Geek sat down. "Whew! What a flake! She can get lost for good as far as I'm concerned."

"If you feel that way, why did you bring her here?"

"It was a snow job. My mother and Jill's grandmother cooked it up between them. I said I had to work, but when the pharmacy closed Jill was there with the tickets and Gam with the car and my mother with my blazer and Grandpa saw that I put it on."

"Well, it's your own fault. You should have asked your own girl months ago."

The Geek gave her a look. "There's only one girl I've ever wanted to take out and she's tied up."

Sherry fidgeted. "There are lots of girls in Pineridge."

The Geek sighed. "Maybe the campus scene will be an improvement."

"Where are you going?" she asked politely.

"I'm shooting for the university, like my father and my grandfather." The Geek rubbed his hand over his chin. "And what about you, Sherry?"

"That depends."

"I suppose when you're really smart it's hard to make up your mind. Not that the university is a pushover."

Sherry sipped her float. Wouldn't The Geek be surprised if she told him that she was dreaming of a cabin in the woods and not a Phi Beta Kappa key? In fact, she was practically flunking out of high school.

The Geek leaned closer. "The university's so big it could be a get-lost town. But if you go there, I'll track you down. Okay?"

"Sure." Sherry saw Kent and Jill at the door and smoothed her dress. It really had been only a minute.

"C'mon, Geekie," Jill said, and The Geek winced. "Treat me to a pizza and then I'll let you off the hook. I've got to pack."

"Well," Sherry said when Jill and The Geek were out the gym door, "what was that all about?"

"Jill gave me a letter."

"Don't you want to read it?"

"She made me promise not to until I'm alone."

"In that case, I don't see why she just couldn't have handed it to you right here."

"I wouldn't know," Kent said, but his face turned red, and at the first blast of the trumpet he pulled her to her feet. "Dance?"

She fitted into his arms but another couple jostled them. Kent missed a step and grabbed her, and the corsage pin pricked her. It was only a little scratch but the pain shot right through to her heart.

NINETEEN

Sherry reached for the note marked "urgent" in her locker. MEET ME AFTER SCHOOL IN THE SECRET PLACE. KENT.

The note could mean only one thing. Jill had made her final farewell. The note banished any lingering doubts, lifting her to the same happy heights as she'd experienced the night of her seventeenth birthday when Kent had entrusted her with his ring. At last he was free. Free of Jill's tyranny, her outrageous demands, and in good conscience could return to the Secret Place that had always been theirs alone.

The Secret Place. They had been here only once this spring, and Kent had promised to come back and clear out the undergrowth. He hadn't, and now Sherry was struck by the lushness of the vegetation. The creepers were longer and tougher, the ferns more abundant, and the mosquitoes legion.

She sat down facing the path, waiting for Kent to round the bend. The big oak would always stand, but when they built their cabin the small pines and popple would be cleared away. But not the birch. The white bark was a bright accent among the dark-trunked, dark-needled conifers.

At last Kent hurrying toward her.

"Can you believe it's grown so wild since the last time we were here?" She smiled.

"No matter. I just needed a place where we won't be overheard."

"This is it. Just the two of us. All the privacy in the world."

Kent sucked in his cheeks, giving his face a morose look.

"Sherry, I hate to do this to you —"

Instantly bad vibes swarmed around her like the swarm of insects overhead.

Kent sat down opposite, but he didn't look at her. He focused on a spot beyond her, like a TV actor reading cue cards. "Now about the letter Jill gave me last night —"

Sherry nodded mechanically as if Kent had jerked a string.

"Well, it wasn't exactly what I expected. Actually it was a Xerox copy of the letter I'd sent her."

Sherry slapped a king-sized mosquito on her arm, but the mosquito hung on and she wondered why she had no strength to kill it. "Do you mean to tell me you've been writing to her, too?" she said.

"Only once. We'd been together all day."

His voice grew strangely excited. "I don't need to tell you how crazy I am about her. It's something I can't help. It's just there. For real. You're no fool, Sherry. I'm sure you've known all along."

In a way she had. But her heart had refused to accept what her mind told her.

Her head began to throb, blow after blow like an ax hacking away at a tree, but she forced the words out. "Are you saying that all the times you've held me and kissed me and made promises, none of it meant anything to you?"

"Of course it did. You know I've tried again and again to get back with you, and when Jill wasn't around I could make myself believe it was like old times. But Jill is very much around. And she's dynamite. I never knew I could get so stirred up over anyone. When I'm near her, my adrenaline pumps up a storm."

Bewitched, Sherry thought. Aloud she said. "You were telling me about the letter . . ."

"We'd parted for the night, but I couldn't sleep. She has a way of getting me all worked up. Well, I wrote her a note. I promised to give her whatever she wanted as a keepsake when it was time for her to leave for Singapore. Now she's calling me on it."

Sherry sat up straight. The stone was hard, unrelenting under her.

"So . . ."

Kent ran his hand through his thick, wavy hair. "I hope you understand."

158

Should she make it easy for him? Should she say that of course she understood? But the truth was she didn't understand. She said nothing.

He took a deep breath and blurted out, "Jill wants my ring."

Sherry stifled the scream that was trying to escape her throat. *No, Kent, no!* She waited, quieting her beating heart.

"Your ring? I thought you gave it to me." Her lips twisted. "*Always*."

"I know. I know." He turned away. Restless hands reached for a vine and yanked it up. How effortlessly he pulls up roots, Sherry thought.

"Let's get this straight." Sherry spoke deliberately, weighing each word. "You say you love Jill. You want her to wear the ring that was a lifetime promise to me."

Kent stammered. "It's — it's up to you, Sherry. I mean I told Jill that I would ask for it, but I was sure that you'd never give the ring up."

The mosquito bite on her arm grew bigger and redder. She felt nothing.

"If it's my ring you want for her," Sherry said with dignity, "look no further."

She stood up and unclasped the gold chain and slipped the ring off the tiny rungs. She tossed it to him. "So much for us!" she said.

"Sherry, don't you see it's hard on me, too?"

Suddenly the stones circling the Secret Place looked like tombstones. HEREIN LIES

BURIED OUR LOVE. Without a backward glance she started down the path.

"Sherry!" Kent caught up with her, putting his arm through hers. "Can't we be friends?"

She shook the arm off and began running. When she reached her house, she shut the door in his face and ran up the long flight of stairs to her room and locked herself in. The turquoise and white soothed. In a trance she walked over to the chest at the foot of the bed and brought out Pooh Bear. She sat down in the rocker and, with Pooh cradled in her arms, rocked and rocked. Looking down in the black, shiny eyes she saw tears that had to be a reflection of her own.

TWENTY

"Sherry Russell, what have you to say for yourself?"

Sherry stood mute, averting her eyes from Miss Hatcher's hostile gaze.

"Have you an explanation for missing your French final yesterday?"

"No."

"You are fully aware of the consequences of your action?"

"Yes."

Miss Hatcher leaned forward in the swivel chair and glared. "Do you mean to tell me that you're letting Kent Halliday ruin your life?"

Sherry gasped.

"I see one ray of hope. His ring is gone."

Sherry's hand flew to her bare throat.

"Oh, yes, I've noticed that ring hanging around your neck like a noose."

Sherry's eyes blazed. "That ring meant a great deal to me, Miss Hatcher."

"I wouldn't say it had done much for you. In the short time you had it, your grades dropped, your health deteriorated, and now you've cut your exam without any excuse whatsoever."

Sherry straightened and said coldly, "It isn't the ring, Miss Hatcher."

"Sit down," Miss Hatcher commanded. "I suppose you're going to tell me that if it hadn't been for Jill Keller you'd still be wearing the ring and life would be beautiful."

Sherry sank slowly into the chair. She felt stunned. That's exactly the way her life could have been, but she didn't need the Hatchet Lady telling her so.

Miss Hatcher rapped her gnarled knuckles on the desk. "Now listen to me, Sherry. You think Kent did you a favor giving you his ring. You were pleased and flattered and it made you feel special. But in reality the ring had a stifling effect. It tied you to him. Just seventeen and no options. Do you really want to be tied for the rest of your life to a boy who is barely making it through school, and then only with your help and now a tutor's?"

"That's not fair, Miss Hatcher." Sherry was surprised to hear herself speak up. It had always been, yes, Miss Hatcher, no, Miss Hatcher. And even though Kent had hurt her deeply, she felt compelled to set the record straight. "Kent doesn't need an academic background. He isn't trying to be a chemist or a doctor or a lawyer or a teacher. When he graduates, he will be working for his father."

"Sherry, many car dealers have gone bankrupt, and if Kent doesn't show any more business acumen than he has so far there's very little hope the Halliday dealership will survive under his management."

"Kent will make a fine mechanic and an excellent salesman," Sherry bristled, "and you don't need to bury his dealership yet."

"So in spite of everything you still champion Kent. My advice then is that if you insist on marrying a boy who is going nowhere the least you can do is prepare yourself."

"Miss Hatcher, Kent and I don't even see each other."

"Mark my words. He'll be back." Miss Hatcher sighed and for an unguarded moment the hatchet face looked vulnerable. "We're living in a very uncertain world, Sherry, where dreams don't necessarily come true."

Dreams, Sherry thought. What did Miss Hatcher know of dreams? Could she have walked through the woods under a June moon that dappled the path in gold? Could she have met a special someone at a Secret Place? Was it possible?

"You're a very lucky young lady," Miss Hatcher said. "Your family is able to send you through college, and you have the capacity to succeed." She pointed a finger. "Now don't blow it!"

"Oh, Miss Hatcher," Sherry whispered, "I already have."

"Oh, I know what a mess you've made of things. But I haven't earned the title Hatchet Lady without cause. I can lower the ax. I can also raise it. I will give you one last chance. You are to go to summer school and make up this last semester. If you do well, the semester will be wiped off your record. If you do poorly, that's it."

"Thank you, Miss Hatcher. Thank you very much."

Sherry stood up. Her father had been right all along. Miss Hatcher could be a friend as well as a foe and only through her benevolence had Sherry been given another chance. Of course the homework would be staggering, but actually she felt relieved. There would be no time to go tooling around the countryside with Kent, even if he asked her to.

TWENTY-ONE

Sherry darted across the landing, past the stained-glass window glowing like a giant ruby in the late daylight, and down the second flight of stairs, slowing when she saw Mom waiting by the newel post.

"Hi, Mom."

"Didn't you tell me you were never going to Block Club again as long as you lived?"

"It's okay, Mom." Sherry slid her hand along the wide oak bannister as she descended the last few steps. "I'm bound to run into him sometime, and this way I'll be with friends. Tina begged me. She said there was something special on the agenda and I simply had to come."

"Sherry . . ."

"Yes?"

"I've been doing some thinking since you gave Kent back his ring."

"Don't hedge, Mom. He asked for it back."

"I'm glad it happened," Mom said with conviction, and Sherry caught her breath.

"But, Mom, I thought you liked Kent!"

"Of course I do. Until these past few months, he's been a very likeable person, and ever since his mother died he's been over here so much I began to look upon him as part of our family circle."

"I know." Sherry's voice was a whisper.

"And when he gave you his ring, there were stars in your eyes. You were so sure."

Sherry felt the pain press her heart, but the pain wasn't as sharp as it had been at first.

"Come, dear, sit down for a minute." Sherry sat on the bottom step and Mom sat beside her. Sherry thought she'd never seen Mom sit on the stairs before.

"Naturally it made us happy," Mom spoke slowly, and Sherry could see that she'd given the matter a great deal of thought, "that you, our only child, were going to marry a boy from Pineridge whose job would keep him here. Dad and I even talked about giving you some property as a wedding present."

Sherry felt the color rush to her cheeks. How close she'd come to asking for a plot of land in the woods! But she hadn't quite done it, nor had Dad made the offer to her.

"You see, Sherry, I liked to picture your life as a continuation of ours."

"That's what I hoped for, too."

"But, Sherry, there's one big difference. Just like you and Kent, your father and I knew each other forever, but as young people we didn't pair off. All of us just had fun together. And when we started dating, he dated other girls, and I went out with other boys.

"But once he gave me his ring, he never looked at another girl. Kent just isn't ready for that kind of a commitment, and frankly you're too young, too. Any mother hates to see her daughter hurt, but thankfully it happened now."

"Mom, don't worry. I'm really excited about going to the university."

"That's the way it should be. But I don't like to see you working so hard over the summer, getting tired."

"But I'm not at all tired," Sherry insisted, and feeling in an expansive mood added, "Ms. Adams — she's the English teacher I like so much — really went for my poem. She said it would lead off the literary section in the yearbook."

"Would you let me read it?" Mom asked tentatively and Sherry thought how few things she'd shared with her mother over the past year.

"Oh, yes! It's called 'The Garden,' but it isn't about gardening. It's about love. Is love a perennial or an annual?"

"Well?"

"Buy the yearbook and read all about it!" Sherry laughed and pushed up from the stair. "I have to go, Mom."

She started down the hall but the water-color caught her attention and she stopped and stared. Like that freak tornado, Jill had swept through Pineridge and changed things. The tornado had lopped off the front porch and leveled the outhouses and toppled the giant beech, but it had forced her great-great-grandfather to rebuild and modernize the house. As devastating as the storm had been, in the long run things were better.

"Will the meeting please come to order?" Tina banged the gavel on the podium. "Will someone please move that the minutes of the last meeting be dispensed with?"

"I so move."

"Any new business?"

Brian jumped up. "I move the meeting be adjourned."

Before Sherry's unbelieving eyes, everyone stood up and filed out.

"Tina," Sherry said, "wait for me!"

But Tina didn't turn, and Kent grabbed her by the arm.

"Don't go, Sherry. I arranged this. I've got to talk to you."

"I wouldn't know why."

"Sherry, please. You won't talk to me on the phone. You shut the door in my face. Don't you think after all the years we've gone together, you owe me just a few minutes?"

Sherry thought, *I owe you nothing*. But she decided to stay.

"Sherry, you have to believe me." His dark eyes pleaded with her. "I've always loved you and there's never been anyone else and there never will be."

"You've forgotten Jill so soon?"

Kent shook his head. "How some crazy girl could get me so mixed up, I'll never understand. She had me jumping through hoops, running when I should have walked, saying things that I never should have said. I was miserable the whole time and now that she's gone, I can honestly say I hardly remember what she even looked like." He lowered his voice. "Sherry, there'd be no way I could spend the rest of my life with someone like Jill. You know me better than that."

"Just one question, then. Why did you give her my ring?"

Kent frowned and for a moment he looked like a little boy lost in the deep woods with no way out.

"I don't know. I don't know." And the funny thing was she believed him.

"I'm really sorry now," he said after a pause, and she saw that he was groping. "The only thing I can say is that in the course of a lifetime everyone makes a mistake and I just hope you're big enough to forgive me."

"Oh, I forgive you."

Kent's face lighted up, the fabulous 1000-watt smile. "Then it's the same? Just the two of us? We'll go ahead with the wedding and the honeymoon and our own little cabin."

Dream cabin. She closed her eyes and saw a dark, damp little house overshadowed by gloomy trees. Instead of a bird song she heard the whine of insects and a clock ticking endlessly through a long, lonely day.

"I said I'd forgive you. But the dream cabin and the dream wedding will have to wait."

"Why?" The smile dimmed.

"I'm going to college."

"So long as you come back weekends" — he slid along the bench toward her — "I'll manage."

"Not that college. I'm going to the university if they'll take me."

"No, Sherry. It's too big. You'd need a spaceship to get around."

"Nevertheless that's where I'm going. For four years. Maybe longer. And then I'd like to go to England and see New Forest with all the ponies running wild and the Tower of London and the chalk cliffs and the moats and the castles and all the things Jill was forever talking about."

Kent straightened. "You expect me to wait four years? Isn't that asking a lot?"

"I don't expect anything from you, Kent. I'm just telling you what I'm doing." She met his eyes. "Why don't you try for college, too? Even if it's only junior college —"

"A waste of time and effort. I'm working for Dad."

"And what happens if your father's business goes on the rocks?"

"It won't."

"You have no alternate plan?"

"What do you mean by that?"

"I mean when the electricity fails, it's nice to have a candle in the house."

"What a dumb thing to worry about."

"It wouldn't have occurred to me a month ago."

"Look," Kent said, "I went to all this trouble to get us together, and now you're throwing all these curves at me — four years of college, traveling after that." The corners of his mouth tightened into a grim line. "I wish I'd never heard of Jill Keller."

It was so easy to lay it all on Jill. That's exactly what she had done and that's what he was doing now. But maybe from the beginning she and Kent were not the team everyone said they were. Because they were neighbors, because he was handsome and she was pretty, because they'd been thrown together, matched up, paired off for so long, they had both come to believe what everyone said — they were made for each other. But were they?

"Don't you love me anymore?" Kent looked white and shaken, just as he had the day of his mother's funeral and Mom had said, *Come home with us, Kent.*

"I don't know. Give me time." It would be all too easy to move back into his arms.

"You said you're going away. Are you coming back?"

"Of course." She'd always come back to this lovely town. Whether she stayed depended on a lot of things. How did she know if she liked the big scene until she tried it? How did she know whether she'd find an exciting new someone at the university or whether Kent would find a new girl the minute she left town or whether time would bring them together again?

"Well, if you're coming back, I want you to have the ring I ordered for you," Kent said.

The word ring chilled her. *Noose*, Miss Hatcher had called it.

"I said I'd come back, but I didn't say I would stay. And I'm not going to wear another one of your class rings. Ever." Her hand went to her throat as it had so many times before, but now it touched the little gold charm that Mrs. Brophy had given her with the inscription on the back, FOR SHERRY, WITH GRATITUDE.

She stood up.

"Aren't you going to kiss me?"

"Of course." She leaned over and gave him a light kiss on the lips. "See you around," she said, hurrying out into the night with the moon sailing above the row of pines. There was no ring around it and she knew it would be beautiful tomorrow.